Dead of Winter

(Battle of the Bulls, Book 2)

T. S. JOYCE

Dead of Winter

ISBN: 9798699494019
Copyright © 2020, T. S. Joyce
First electronic publication: October 2020

T. S. Joyce
www. tsjoyce.com

NOTE FROM THE AUTHOR:

This book is a work of fiction. The names, characters, places, and incidents are products of the writer's imagination or have been used fictitiously and are not to be construed as real. Any resemblance to persons, living or dead, actual events, locale or organizations is entirely coincidental. The author does not have any control over and does not assume any responsibility for third-party websites or their content.

Published in the United States of America

First digital publication: October 2020
First print publication: October 2020

DEDICATION

For Wrangler jeans.

Thank you for what you do for booty cheeks.

ACKNOWLEDGMENTS

You readers have done more for me and my stories than I can even explain on this teeny page. You found my books, and ran with them, and every share, review, and comment makes release days so incredibly special to me.

1010 is magic and so are you.

ONE

"Are you sure you belong here?"

Raven stopped shifting her weight from foot to foot and twisted around. "Me?" she asked the woman standing behind her in line for the beer truck.

The pretty woman was dressed in bootcut jeans, muddy boots, and a flannel shirt that she'd tied just below her perky boobs. Her tight midriff was exposed. She had platinum locks cascading down her shoulders from under her white felt cowboy hat.

Blondie was the complete opposite of Raven.

"You sure have a lot of tattoos." The woman scrunched up her face. "You would be so cute if you hadn't done that to your skin."

Stunned, Raven glanced down at herself. Black

ripped-up shorts, black motorcycle boots, black tank top, and a red and black Harley Davidson flannel tied around her waist. And yep, she had tattoos—a sleeve of them down her right arm and all down her left leg.

Raven's cheeks were burning. Shyness was a beast she still hadn't figured out how to deal with. She didn't know how to respond, so she said awkwardly, "Umm, I just like tattoos and how they look."

"Huh," the girl said. "Are you here to see the riders or the bulls?"

Okay, friendly conversation. The woman wasn't going to make her feel like an outsider anymore, so this was good. She parted her lips to answer, but the girl's eyes went wide and she took a step back.

"Your eyes. They just went from light green to brown. I know what that means." She looked around as if checking to see if any of the rodeo-goers around them were paying attention to her discovery. Louder, she called out, "I know what changing eye colors mean!"

"Okay," Raven murmured, stepping forward in line to put in her order. "Think I need two beers," she told the cashier of the little booze truck parked outside the rodeo arena.

"Are you with one of the bulls? Are you a girlfriend? You're a cow shifter, right?" the girl asked from way too close behind her.

Inside of Raven, her animal stirred. *It's okay, it's okay, it's okay.* Cow shifter sounded lame, but her animal was a monster. Purebred Texas Longhorn shifter and full of fury when she took the skin, so... "Can you give me a little space?" Raven whispered. "Please?"

"Right, right," Blondie said, throwing her hands up and backing away a maximum of three inches. Freakin' humans.

"Are you with one of the bulls? I'm a huge fan of Quickdraw Slow Burn. I came here to cheer for him. I follow him on social media. He has an eight-pack." Blondie was staring down at her phone.

"Here you go," the cashier said with a friendly smile as he set two plastic cups of frothy light beer on the counter. "That'll be ten bucks even."

Raven pulled a ten-dollar bill out and then two more dollars to put into the tip jar beside the register. "Hey, thanks mister."

"It's so weird to hear a country drawl on a goth

chick," Blondie said. "Okay, here." She shoved her phone at Raven just as Raven was turning around with both beers in hand. She jerked to a stop and spilled a little. Blondie was showing her a picture from Quickdraw's Instagram page. A picture Raven had already seen because she'd stalked all the bulls being represented by Cheyenne Walker.

"This is who you're with, right? He is covered in tattoos, too. Y'all would match."

"I don't know him," Raven murmured, staring at the background of the picture. The background was more important than the giant, muscled-up, black-haired behemoth cheering behind the chutes at the second event of the Battle of the Bulls circuit. Behind him was the man she'd come to see. The one who had caught her attention from the moment the news broke that he had a human mother.

Dead of Winter was standing behind Quickdraw, screaming, gripping the top of a gate behind the chutes. He'd been cheering on Two Shots Down, who was bucking during the taking of this picture.

"Damn, I totally thought I had you pegged."

"Nope. Just here as a fan. Like you," Raven assured her and walked around the nosy human.

Are you sure you belong here?

She looked around at the cowboy boots, the hats, the Wranglers, the belt buckles, and gripped her beers a little tighter as she stepped around a giant pile of horse crap in the middle of the walkway.

Hell no, she didn't belong here, at some rodeo in Boise, Idaho.

She didn't belong anywhere.

TWO

"You don't belong here."

Dead of Winter charged First Time Train Wreck and just barely missed the bull shifter in his human skin when he scurried up the alleyway fence. He rammed where the heckler had disappeared and dented in that length of fencing. Across the alleyway, his agent, Cheyenne, was yelling profanities at Train Wreck. Little hellion woman didn't like anyone messing with their heads right before a big buck.

As a kid, he'd always wanted a guard dog. Who the hell would've ever thought he would get one in the form of a five-foot-six mouthy woman?

The handlers were behind him with hot shots in their hands, threatening him to move forward by the pulsating electric current on the ends of the long wands.

First Time Train Wreck, watch your back tonight. I'm gonna find you after you buck.

He bolted forward, his hooves sinking into the alleyway dirt. The crowd outside was cheering a deafening sound. He trotted to the end of the alley and loaded into chute number two. The handlers closed him in, and this was the part he hated—the before. The cage. The waiting. The few minutes before a buck where a rider had to settle on his back and he was trapped under that human's weight and spurs. The clang of a fence made him flinch back, and he slammed his horn against the gate hard. The gateman was ready, holding the rope attached to the gate taught, weight on his back leg, eyes boring through the slats of the gate at Dead. Dead had trampled him before, but the old coot had learned his lesson. Now, he always got out of the way fast. Pity.

Dunbar Cooper was settling onto his back now, his spurs running painfully down Dead's ribs as he eased his legs on either side of his back. Dead held still. For now. Quickdraw was loading two chutes down, ready to buck after Dead. He was kicking and headbutting the rails, making a mess of his rider's head. That was his favorite move in the chutes.

Dead's? He liked to stay still, and then when the rider got comfortable and distracted, he would screw with him. The announcer was telling the huge crowd Dead's entire life story. God, he hated this part of the circuit now. All the research into his past, all the rumors, all the conversation about who he really was. Right now, they were talking about his mother, the human, the vessel for this monster bull shifter, and blah blah blah. Too bad Mom didn't mean to be a vessel for a bull shifter. Too bad she'd done her best to cut the animal right out of Dead. *But go ahead, Mr. Announcer. Talk about her like she's worth a damn.* Talk about her like Dead hadn't gotten himself here by his own bootstraps with no help from anyone, especially not his mother. That's what humans did. They took the credit away from the animals. *Of course*, the announcers would give credit to his human mom.

Dunbar's spur dug into his side harder, and Dead reared back and slammed him against the gate. The rider yelled but held. Little barnacle. He was going to be tough to buck. Dunbar had been making a run and had some confidence in him now.

Cheyenne and Two Shots Down's voices echoed through his head. They were here now and riled up on his behalf. Protective herd.

Cheyenne was ripping on the flankman for putting the rope on Dead's nuts, and Two Shots was leaning down into the chute, yelling at him to, "Buck up, Dead! Train Wreck will take your place if you don't put Dunbar on the ground. No mercy. Get rid of him!"

Adrenaline pumped through his body. Dead looked out through the slats to the arena again. Gateman was ready, pickup men were ready across the dirt clearing, the bullfighters were all tensed and waiting.

A man laced a rope through the chute slats and flung it around his head behind his horns but in front of the muscular hump on his back. Shit. They did this when there wasn't enough fight in a bull. Dead hated the feel of the rope sliding back and forth, back and forth on his neck. He slammed his body against the gate, but still the rope rubbed, back and forth, back and forth.

Thunderstruck blared over the loudspeakers, and

he could feel Dunbar nod to the gateman.

The second the gateman pulled the rope and it released from his neck, and Dead flew out of the chute. When his front hooves hit the dirt, he kicked high, pushing Dunbar perpendicular so he would slam down on his hand that was holding the rope.

He twisted on the next buck, tossing his head the opposite direction of his body. He needed his hurt shoulder to hold tonight. His tight, quick spins wouldn't work on Dunbar. He needed the power behind his landings and kicks to rid himself of this tick of a human.

Rage fueled him as his hooves hit the ground again, throwing a cloud of dirt up. Cameras were flashing, the crowd was screaming, Dunbar's team was shouting for him to stay on, Cheyenne and Two Shots were yelling for him to throw his rider, and then it happened, like it always did. The sound died to nothing, and the flashback began. The torture. The needles. Mom staring at him stone-faced through the window glass of some sterile room. The attempted assassination of an animal that refused to die. The flashback of the pain dumped more adrenaline into him. The echoes of his own screaming filled his head, and he slammed back to earth, twisted, rose back up, and kicked in the air. When he landed, Dunbar went flying forward and hit the dirt on his back.

Dead could hear the wind leave his lungs, but he didn't care if the rider was down. He didn't care about the buzzer that signified Dead had bucked him off in time. He didn't care about anything but killing that motherfucking human because, in this body, humans would always be evil. In this body, he would always hate them. In this body, he would always be scared, and for a creature like Dead...fear manifested as violence.

Dunbar couldn't get away fast enough. Dead's black heart smiled as he aimed for him. The bullfighters were yelling, hitting his face then ducking out of the way, and Dead fell for a couple of their moves. One was dragging Dunbar away while two other fighters were trying to get his attention away from Dunbar.

Too slow. He slung his head and knocked one of them off his feet. At the gap he created, he closed in on Dunbar in a few steps. He slammed his horn against the rider's chest, jerked his head and slung him against Quickdraw's chute gate.

Cheyenne was screaming something, Two Shots, too, but fuck their words. They didn't understand how cruel the humans were. They didn't understand the necessity for revenge. They didn't understand that he had to do this to feel okay. To feel steady.

The bullfighters were good, but not good enough. They were touching his nose, charging him, two working as one, but Dead only had eyes for the rider on the ground. He tossed his head and bolted the last few steps. So close to the limp cowboy. So close.

Two Shots jumped down from the top of the chute and threw his body over Dunbar, who wasn't moving.

He should kill Two just for taking that from him. Should kill him for protecting that human.

He should.

He would.

Cheyenne jumped from the top of the fence, slammed down into the dirt in front of Two Shots, and threw her hands over her face.

Shit, he couldn't stop. He couldn't stop! Too much weight behind him, too fast, too much power.

Cheyenne!

Dead jumped at the last moment to avoid her and

slammed into Quickdraw's gate. He tried his best to avoid the pile of bodies, but there wasn't enough space. His hooves slammed down on Two Shot's leg.

Dead trotted away, feeling like there was poison in his guts. Two. Two, Two, Two. He was limping while he and Cheyenne dragged Dunbar's limp body with the bullfighters.

Fuck the limping rider, but Two was limping, too. Had Dead broken Two's legbone?

He trotted around the curve of the arena fences, but it wasn't his usual victory lap. His eyes were on Two, on his face as he winced in pain with each step and had trouble climbing out of the arena. Dead slowed and stopped, head up, ears erect, eyes on Two. Two, Two, Two, his friend Two. Part of his herd.

"It's okay," a woman said softly near him.

Her voice was as clear as a bell over the roaring of the crowd. What? Dead ripped his gaze from Two's disappearing back and looked up into eyes as black as night. Black eyes, black hair, pink tinted cheeks, black clothes and tattoos painting her skin. She leaned forward and said it again and, this time, the words moved right through him. "It's okay."

A rope flung in front of his face and made him

15

flinch when it landed on his neck. It tightened, and then a second landed on his neck before he could back up. The pickup men were here to take him from the arena since he hadn't gone through the exit gates on his own. As they dragged him toward the open gate between two of the chutes, he locked his legs, tried to keep his eyes on the girl. The girl who stuck out like a sore thumb. The only girl still sitting in her seat while everyone else was up, cheering and jeering. The only one who'd been speaking quietly just to him.

It's okay.

No, Girl Who Didn't Belong.

His entire life, he'd stayed away from close relationships, because he hadn't wanted to be hurt ever again, and now he'd hurt Two. Two, his friend. Two, his herd. Two who had to buck in two weeks and keep his rank so this herd could stay together, and Dead had just landed on his leg.

It wasn't okay.

THREE

Raven fidgeted with the VIP pass around her neck. "Two more please," she asked the cashier at the booze truck.

"You can sure put the beer away," he said. Oh, she knew he was teasing from the sparkle in his eyes, but she didn't want him to think bad of her. "I'm getting one for someone else."

"Ten bucks again," he said as he set the plastic cups on the counter.

She paid and made her way carefully back toward the chutes. There was a VIP entrance there. This pass had cost her an arm and a leg, but when else would she get a chance to meet him? To meet Dead of Winter, the badass number three bull in the world.

Well...number four now. He'd just dropped a rank tonight. Some bull shifter named First Time Train Wreck had outscored him, but she didn't really understand any of the technicalities of this sport. Dead had bucked his rider off before the buzzer, so why the heck did he get dropped a rank? Everyone in the arena had gone wild when he'd bucked and gone after his rider.

Dunbar Whatever-His-Name-Was had recovered. He'd just been knocked out. He'd come out behind the chutes and watched some of the other riders after a few minutes. That was good. At least, Dead hadn't killed him, but she'd watched the huge black and white bull's eyes. They had stayed on his teammates, not the rider. He hadn't cared much about what happened to Dunbar. Something was wrong with that bull. She had to know if the man was as monstrous.

She passed under the VIP sign and made her way down a narrow alleyway, showed the man at the end of it the pass that hung around her neck, and asked where she was supposed to go.

"Right there some of the bulls and riders will be signing autographs," he said, gesturing to a row of tables against a wall.

"Thank you so much," she said quietly.

A couple of pretty girls on horses trotted through the alleyway so Raven pressed her shoulders against the wall to stay out of the way of those hooves. She didn't know anything about horses, or rodeos, or any of the events she'd just seen, but she'd enjoyed herself. This was a completely different world than she was used to.

Careful not to spill the beers, she made her way to where other VIP members were gathering around the tables. A few of the tables already had riders at them, signing autographs for lines of people. The three closest to her were labeled Quickdraw Slow Burn, Two Shots Down, and Dead of Winter on a place tag written with pink glittery ink. She didn't know why that made her giggle, but it did. Those boys didn't look like the pink sparkly type.

There were already lines in front of the bulls' tables. She stood in Dead of Winter's line behind a trio of excited cowgirls for a few minutes, but the beer was getting warm, and everyone who was anyone knew warm beer was gross.

So, she meandered away from the crowd and peeked through a doorway the signing riders had come through. In the hallway were none other than Dead of Winter and Cheyenne Walker. They were talking low, but cow shifters had amazing hearing, so she could make out what they were saying just fine.

"He's going to be fine, Dead. Kicking yourself isn't an excuse to skip out on the signing."

"Well, Quickdraw doesn't have to do it."

"Yes, he does! You all have to do it. That's part of the contract."

Dead threw up his hands and sauntered off. "Tell them to take it out of my paycheck. I'm not going to take some dumb pictures with a bunch of humans. I've had a shit night, Cheyenne. I'm not even a top three bull anymore, so I don't really think my contract sticks."

"Yeah, but in two weeks you'll be back in the top three!" Cheyenne yelled after him. "This is just a bump in the road! We will train harder!"

"I don't need to train harder! I need to grow my beard back. That's probably where my power came from."

"Your beard?" Cheyenne asked with a snort.

"Yeah! And you come along and make me trim it for stupid social media and to look like some pretty boy for the lady fans, and I don't care about any of that. I liked being hairy!"

"Yeah, I'm aware, Dead! Your constant pictures of your hairy legs say as much, but you look much more handsome now."

"I want to look like a mountain man. I'm never listening to you again," he grumbled. "I'm going home."

"Your home is a camper."

"Then I'm going to my camper. I have to lick my wounds in private and drown my sorrows in cheap beer."

And that was Raven's que. She cleared her throat and called out softy, "Excuse me?"

Dead stopped in his tracks and twisted around and, good golly, that man was something to look at. He was tall as a mountain, wide as a barn, and had bright green eyes, even brighter than her own. He was wide in the chest and trim in the waist and wore a charcoal gray T-shirt that emphasized his ripped physique. He wore jeans with mud smears, and his sandy brown hair was all messy on top. Maybe he'd ran his hands through it a bunch, or maybe he'd spent time in the mirror getting it to stand up like that. She didn't know. All she knew is he was the most striking man she'd ever seen.

"Yeah?" he asked.

Raven swallowed hard. *Be brave, little cow.* She lifted up a beer. "It's getting a little warm, but I got a beer for you."

He frowned but then sidled Cheyenne in the narrow hallway, approaching Raven. "I know you."

"Oh, no, not me. I've never been to one of these things before."

"You've never been to a shifter bull riding event?"

She shook her head and held out the cup of beer. "I don't even own a pair of boots."

Dead hooked his hands on his hips and narrowed his eyes. "Motorcycle boots count as boots."

Raven stared at the toes of her black leather boots. "Oh. I guess that's true." She cleared her throat again and murmured, "Here." She shook the beer a little that she was still holding in her outstretched hand.

Dead closed the last few feet between them and, holy bull balls, he was so much bigger up close. She had to stretch her neck all the way up to look him in the face.

His eyes were narrowed and suspicious. "Are you trying to roofie me?"

"W-what?" she stammered. "No! Of course not."

"Dammit. That would've been fun."

"Dead!" Cheyenne admonished. "It's not okay to make roofie jokes!"

"Warden," he called over his shoulder, "have you ever met a cow shifter before?"

Raven's heart got sucked straight up into her throat, and she froze.

"Uuuuh, no," Cheyenne Walker murmured, walking toward them.

"Because this little stick of dynamite smells like a cow."

Now self-conscious, Raven sniffed herself, but she just smelled like she always did.

Dead snatched the beer from her hand and tinked it against her own beer, then intertwined their arms like they were drinking champagne at their wedding. "Ready?" he asked.

"What are you doing?" she asked, leaning as far back from him as possible.

"We are chugging this together."

"Why?" she squeaked out. "W-why would you

want to drink like this?"

"Because you said 'it's okay.'"

Oooooh, he did recognize her from the arena. Clearly, his human side was present when he was in his bull form.

"Ready?" he asked.

"Uuuuummm..."

"To nearly breaking my best friend's leg, trying to kill a rider, and almost dropping to fourth place and breaking up my herd."

"Uuuuh, cheers?" To the weirdest toast ever.

Arm hooked in his, she drank her beer, but not fast enough. Dead of Winter slammed his back and even spilled some as he gulped it in just a few swallows. And then he had time to tell her, "Come on girl, get it down! Chug it!"

And she did. She spilled it a little and was embarrassed, but when she looked up, he had the biggest grin on his face. And a silly little piece of her glowed with pride. Over drinking a beer? Her life was really strange tonight.

"Want me to sign your boob?"

"Wh-what?" she yelped.

"Dead!" Cheyenne exclaimed. "You can't ask girls

that!"

"Why not? Most of them ask me to sign their boobs. 'It's Okay' seems a little shy. Figured I would ask her first and then she doesn't have to muster up the nerve."

Cheyenne's whiskey-colored eyes were round as moons. "I'm so sorry for his behavior. What's your name again?"

"Cow shifter," Dead answered for her.

"Zip it, Dead. No more words," Cheyenne growled.

Okay, they were kind of funny. "Um, my name is Raven."

"Haaaa!" Dead laughed. "A cow named Raven. This is awesome."

Cheyenne snapped her fingers at the exit and glared at Dead. "Go. I know what you're doing. You've being awful so I won't make you sign autographs tonight. You win! Go check on Quickdraw."

Dead arched his eyebrows up high, and his lips thinned to small lines under that hotboy beard. "On second thought, I want to sign autographs. Me and Raven the Cow are going to sign them together."

"Um, I'm good," Raven said softly. She tried to unhook their arms, but Dead, smooth-as-you-like, grabbed her hand and hooked it into the crook of his elbow.

"I feel like starting some rumors tonight," he said, staring at Cheyenne.

"You know what?" Cheyenne said loud enough to echo down the hallway. "Go do it then. Do whatever you want. Go start some media circus. Go spiral, but it doesn't take away from what's really happening!"

"And what's that?"

"You're upset over Two Shots, and you're spiraling over dropping a rank. You're still part of the herd, Dead! Dropping a rank doesn't matter to me or to Quickdraw or Two. You're still one of us."

"Go check on your mate," Dead murmured. "Me and Raven have boobies to sign."

"But I don't want to sign any boobies," she quietly assured him as he pulled her toward the signing tables.

"Come on, girlfriend."

"I'm not anyone's girlfriend! Oh, my gosh."

She swallowed hard when they got to the doorway. The VIP crowd had grown, and they all looked at her and Dead in the mouth of the entrance. Her cheeks caught fire. "I'm gonna go see about a thing and go bury myself in a hole and never come out again," she murmured, releasing his arm.

She tried to duck to the side and make her escape, but Dead grabbed her hand in his, intertwined their fingers—intertwined them!—and then waved at a group who were snapping pictures. The line at his table was cheering.

"Shoot me with a water gun," she uttered on a breath.

"This is my girlfriend, Raven," Dead announced.

"I actually just met him," she said as he dragged her straight through the crowd toward his table.

"She is a moo cow shifter."

"It's actually just called a cow shifter."

"Her name is Raven and her mother is a pirate and her father is a seaman who works on a crab boat."

"They're both schoolteachers."

"Who teach bomb diffusing in the Netherlands."

"Um, sixth grade math and English in Idaho?"

"And she has an announcement to make about how big my dick is."

"I have no knowledge of his dick size!"

He yanked the chair away from Quickdraw's table

27

and set it gallantly beside his, then gestured for her to take a seat. "My queen."

"I've never wanted to kill a stranger before now," she muttered under her breath, frowning at the boxes of magnets and bookmarks and pictures of Dead that filled open boxes under the table.

"That feeling won't fade with me." Dead arched his eyebrow up higher and pulled her seat back a little. "Have a seat, Sugar Tits."

Raven eyed the exit. All she had to do was make it across an alleyway of trotting horses with riders, bolt under the VIP sign, and then leave the way she came in. Just with two less beers. She was still holding her empty cup.

"Have a seat, have a seat, have a seat," Dead started chanting, and to her utter dismay, the line in front of them started chanting the same.

If the earth opened up right now and swallowed her whole, she'd had a good long run at life and would be fine with it.

Cheyenne was standing off to the side, arms crossed over her chest, frown furrowing her forehead. *I'm so sorry*, she mouthed to Raven.

Me, too, Raven mouthed right back.

Living a literal nightmare, which was to have people's attention on her, she sat in the chair and wished she could bury her head in the sand like an ostrich.

The table got rushed by the first three girls in line, who all had pictures of Dead. Two were glossy eight-by-tens of his black and white bull mid-buck, his back hooves kicked up in the air, while the other one was of him without a shirt on, Wranglers, belt buckle, and a horse saddle thrown over his back. Now, Raven had never been a fan of cowboy hats because they just weren't her style, but on Dead of Winter? He looked sexy. In the picture, a sheen of sweat glistened on his muscular chest, and he had his chin tilted up as he gave the camera a wicked smile.

"You like that one?" he asked as he signed the first one with a silver permanent marker.

"Me?" she asked.

"Yeah you. You keep starin' at it. It's okay to tell your boyfriend he's hot. I like compliments. Compliments and positive reinforcement make me work harder. For example..." He looked up at his fan and grinned at her. "If a woman told me she liked something in the bedroom, I would explore everything about that until she was moaning my name and begging me to never stop."

The fan started fanning herself with a sign that read—Raven leaned forward and squinted at the upside-down words—*Dead, Dead, you're good in bed.*

Oh, God. "I should really be going," Raven whispered.

"Nonsense, you aren't going anywhere," Dead rumbled, squeezing her leg under the table.

She didn't even flinch. Huh. It actually was a little comfort. Huh.

"Look, when you're in a relationship—" he started.

"We aren't in a relationship," she gritted out through clenched teeth.

Dead held up a finger and winked at the next fan, then yanked Raven's chair right up against his and leaned into her ear. "You support your person. Tonight, I have to sign a bunch of half-naked pictures of myself for these humans. I don't like humans much. And I have to take pictures I don't want to take and fill these ladies' spank banks with the fantasy of me, when in reality, I just dropped to a rank that guts me, I'm worried about my friend, I'm drowning in guilt,

I'm starving, my shoulder is sore because I can't seem to keep the damn thing in its socket, and the only thing that has felt decent tonight is when a woman I've never met before said 'It's okay,' in that arena. Support me here, and I'll buy you a pair of boots."

Raven parted her lips to respond, but no words came out. He was just lingering by her ear, his lips almost touching her lobe. She could feel the featherlight wind from his warm breath, and chills rippled up her forearms. "What kind of boots?"

"Western, of course."

"I don't wear cowgirl boots."

"They'll be leather, good quality, and I'll find them in black with a little bit of a heel to show off those sexy legs of yours. Python if you want. I could see you liking snakeskin boots. They match your style. The next rodeo you come to see me at, you'll be wearing the right shoes."

Well, she didn't plan on attending any more rodeos, but how the heck was she going to argue with that? Those boots sounded awesome. And he'd paid attention to her style. Maybe trying black cowgirl boots wouldn't be so bad. If they were a gift and she didn't have to pay for them.

Raven cleared her throat and smiled at the fan who was waiting on the other side of the table, snapping pictures of them with her phone. "Would you like a complimentary magnet of Dead's bull?"

"Atta girl," Dead murmured, easing back. He winked at her—*winked*, like hot boys did in the movies—and then began conversing with his line again.

A few fans later, Cheyenne came up behind them and set two ice waters on the table. She leaned into Raven and whispered, "There is a money box under the table with some change. The pictures are ten bucks apiece if anyone wants to buy one for Dead to sign. The rest of the swag is free. I usually do this for all the boys, but Two Shots can't sign tonight. Quickdraw is coming out any second, so I can handle his table if you are up for working Dead's."

"She ain't workin' it," Dead said. "She's gonna just have fun with me and all these lovely ladies tonight. This table is the party table. How you doin' tonight?" he asked a woman approaching from the front of the line.

Cheyenne rolled her eyes heavenward. "Raven, if you need anything, I'll be floating back and forth between here and Two Shots' room."

"Is he okay?" Raven whispered.

"He will be. There is a vet in with him now."

"He changed?" Dead asked.

"He had to turn bull so they could make sure the bone didn't snap. They think it's just a deep bone bruise, though. Stop worrying, Dead. He's not fragile." Cheyenne shoved him in the back of the head.

"Disagree," he muttered as he signed another picture.

After Cheyenne left, Raven got into the rhythm of it, and really? No one paid much attention to her. For the most part, she got to keep her cloak of invisibility, setting up little gift bags of swag, taking money for pictures, and lining everything up in order so Dead could sign one stack and then move onto the other as he talked to his followers. She even got efficient at taking pictures for people who wanted them with Dead. They would hand her their phones and she would snap a few and, after an hour, she pretty much had it down.

She and Dead made a good team for a couple of strangers. Two times, before they took their seats after pictures, he patted her on the butt as if he knew her. And once she signed a napkin for a very shy fan who said she liked Raven's tattoos. About ten times, the giant, intimidating, bull monster named Quickdraw Slow Burn stared at her with confusion in his dark eyes from the next table down as he signed autographs. She got it. She was confused, too.

She didn't belong here.

An hour and a half in, and Cheyenne told them it was time for Dead to do his interviews.

"But we still have a line," Raven murmured, gesturing to the fifteen or so fans still waiting to talk to Dead.

"Yeah, I don't give a shit about the interviews. These ladies have been waiting a while," Dead rumbled between jokes with a blond-haired beauty with a megawatt smile.

Cheyenne's dark eyebrows drew down. "Buuuut, you always tell me to let you know when you can stop signing. You hate doing this stuff."

"Well, tonight I want to get through the line," he said with a shrug.

Cheyenne's frown morphed into a grin. Pointing at Raven, she said, "You did this."

"What? What did I do?"

"You're doing magic. Dead is always a shit about the work after an event. Good job, gold star," she said as she walked away. "A plus! I'll push Dead's interviews back to last."

The line went fast, and Raven started organizing the small amount of remaining swag into one box as Dead went to talk to Quickdraw, who was also getting ready to leave. Her ears picked up just about anything so she could hear their conversation just fine.

Dead asked, "Did you see him?"

"God, you're like a mother hen," Quickdraw muttered. "He'll be fine. It was an accident."

"Yeah, I accidentally tried to kill a rider and hurt Two instead."

"Who's the girl?" Quickdraw asked low.

"Met her tonight. Name's Raven."

"Shifter?" Quickdraw was looking mighty busy stacking his leftover magnets just so.

"What's it to you?" Dead asked, his voice darkening.

Quickdraw straightened up and looked down his nose at Dead. Then he looked at Raven. Then back at Dead. "A human won't survive you, asshole. My concern is for her. Not you."

"Cow shifter," Raven said, and damn her voice for shaking. "Purebred longhorn."

"The fuck?" Dead asked, twisting toward her in a blur. He and Quickdraw wore matching shocked expressions. It would've been funny if it really *really* wasn't funny.

Every shifter reacted the same way when they found out what she was. She didn't make any sense.

"Well, hell then," Quickdraw muttered, clapping Dead on the back. "I'm not worried about her anymore. I'm worried about you."

Time for a subject change. "That was interesting," she told him.

Dead blinked hard and closed the space between them. "You mispronounced 'fun.'" He took the box from her hands. "A longhorn? For real?"

She snorted and nodded her head, looked at the ground so he wouldn't see the heat in her cheeks. The last thing on earth she liked talking about was her inner animal. "It was really nice to meet you."

"You, too. But if you're saying your goodbyes, it ain't time for that yet. We still have interviews."

"In front of cameras? No."

He hooked his hands on his hips and searched her eyes. As much as she wished she wasn't so affected by the bright green in his eyes, the perfect shade of brown of his hair, his tan skin, or muscles curving against his T-shirt... As much as she wished she wasn't awed by the curve of his smile, the white of his teeth, or the thickness of his manly beard... As much as she wished she wasn't struck by his powerful stance or his ability to look her right in the eye and hold her gaze...she absolutely was. "Please don't ask me to do the interviews."

"I won't make you do the cameras. I think you don't like that attention."

"Nope. Not at all. Not even one percent."

He dropped his gaze to her arm. "But you tattooed your skin. If you don't want people looking at you, why did you decorate yourself like this?"

"I did that for me. I wanted to like what I saw when I looked in the mirror, and I think tattoos are beautiful."

"Hmm," he said softly with a nod of his head. "Well, I think they're beautiful now, too. Maybe someday you can tell me what they all mean."

She didn't know why that made her sad. Perhaps

it was the realization that tonight would end soon. "Yeah. Maybe someday. Hey, Dead?" she asked as he turned to walk away.

"Yeah?"

She bit her lip and looked at where the line of fans had been. "I was supposed to be one of those girls tonight."

He shook his head. "What girls?"

"The ones standing in line to spend a couple minutes with you. Maybe get something signed, but really I just wanted to ask you a question."

The toe of his boot hit a clump of dirt as he adjusted his weight and settled the box under one arm. "What question did you want to ask?"

Be brave. "Your mom is human."

She could hear him swallow hard, and his voice lost some of its luster. "Yeah."

Be brave, be brave, be brave. She forced her gaze from his boots to look him in the eyes when she asked, "So how did you learn how to be a bull?"

The muscles in his face relaxed, and he just stared at her like he was looking right into her soul. "Who're your parents, Raven?"

"That's not why I came he—"

"Who?" he asked again.

Raven shrugged. "I'm adopted."

"By humans?"

She nodded.

"Shit, girl." He scratched the corner of his lip and got a faraway look before he repeated that softer. "Shit, girl."

"I'm just... I guess I'm just..."

"Trying to learn."

"Y-yes. Trying to learn."

"How to be goddamn longhorn."

"You ever feel stuck between two worlds?" she asked on a breath.

He dragged those darkening eyes down her throat to her chest, then to her arms, stomach, legs...motorcycle boots. "Sometimes. Most the time, no. I picked. I chose the bull when I was twelve. I don't call myself half-human. I'm shifter, that's it." He jerked his chin up toward the rodeo arena behind her. "That announcer can say all he wants about my human side, but the truth is, there is no human side. My choice."

He set the box back on the table and leaned against it, eyes on her...always eyes on her. "Did your adoptive parents understand you?"

"They tried their best."

"Mmm. Do you have any friends who are shifters?"

"Yes."

"Another cow? Or a bull?"

"No. Wolf."

He huffed a humorless laugh and clutched the edges of the table he'd sat on. His strong triceps flexed with the movement. "Well, aren't you interesting? A cow named Raven who thinks she's human. What color is your animal?"

"I don't think that's appropriate to—"

"Rule number one to being a cow shifter? There's no shame in your animal, and you sure as hell shouldn't want to hide her. What color?"

"Black."

"Black and...?"

She pursed her lips, but he asked again. "Black and what?"

Her voice barely sounded like anything as she whispered, "Just black."

"Holy fuckin' shit." Dead stood and laughed so loud it echoed through the empty space. "What's your last name, Raven?"

"O'Connor."

"No, I mean what's your real last name?"

Why was she shaking? Why was her heart pounding so hard? She couldn't speak. Didn't want to. She'd come here to ask him questions and maybe understand herself better, not be interrogated on stuff she didn't want to discuss. Ever.

"Forget it." Raven turned and made her way for the exit. This had been a bad idea. A really bad idea.

"Did they brand you?"

Those four words froze her in her tracks. Her feet turned to cement blocks, and she couldn't move.

He was coming closer. Dead. She could feel him and hear him. Closer and closer until he lifted the hem of her black tank top from her low-rise shorts, exposing the top of that awful, ugly brand that took up most of her right hip.

She thought he would replace her tank top and walk away, spitting in disgust. Boys didn't like girls with scars like this.

"You're a Hagan," he murmured, tracing the H with the tip of his finger. "The sixth calf of a Hagan pair." He traced the six. And then he traced the circle

41

that overlapped them. "The only heifer."

"The shame," she said, plastering a smile on her face and turning toward him. "Hagans don't like having girls."

"I know." His eyes tightened at the corners. "Don't make you less valuable. The assholes who brought you into this world did you a favor by dumping you. Stick around this shifter rodeo circuit long enough, and you'll learn that down to your bones."

"What do you mean they did me a favor?"

"Any part longhorn bucker in the circuit will know your lineage just from your brand. Everyone knows the Hagan breeders. That's all they are, Raven. They're breeders. Those herds are run by shifter stock contractors who don't have any ethics. They make money on breeding the meanest, gnarliest bucking bulls. And not just for rodeos. You ever hear of the Bull Fights?"

Raven shook her head. Most of this was news to her.

"Rodeo ain't the only way a mean bull can make a living. Underground fighting is even bigger than this circuit. They just hide it from the humans. For now. Their human sides? Killers. Psychopaths. That's the cost of being the best at bad deeds. I've never even met a half-Hagan that was salvageable, but you? You seem okay. You don't smell head-sick, you don't feel off, you don't even have my bull rankled around you, and I can imagine what kind of beasty you turn into. That makes me think it ain't just genetics in that Hagan lineage that make them bad. Those baby bulls go into training young."

"Training?"

"Gotta mean 'em up. Make 'em rank, make them live up to the name. Do you understand what I'm saying?"

"I...I think so."

Dead gripped her hip right over the brand and pulled her closer. "None of your brothers are okay in any way now, but you are. Do you know what they do to Hagan baby girls most of the time?"

She shook her head, her heart in her throat.

"They cull them. But not your parents. Or maybe it was just your momma doing it behind your daddy's back. She didn't cull you, Raven. She gave you to some humans, and that probably gave you some awful-feeling moments being left like that, but you know what?"

Her eyes burned with the tears that were welling up, threatening to spill over. "What?"

"You're still here." A small smile curved up his lips. "You won."

FOUR

You won.

Just like that, a stranger had taken away the sting of twenty-eight years of uncertainty.

You won.

His revelations about the Hagans had unfurled a wave of chills through her stomach, and for the first time in her life, she felt grateful she'd been left behind. That she'd been abandoned. She had more understanding now in one conversation with Dead than she had in a hundred conversations with her adoptive parents.

You won.

His words had shaken something loose in her middle. Something that had been all cramped up and uncomfortable for as long as she could remember.

She swiveled and studied her brand in the bathroom mirror. H6O. She'd only figured out the H meant she was from a Hagan herd, but that bloodline had so many members in the world. And the information about Hagans was so guarded and secretive, she'd been spinning her wheels for years trying to learn anything about them.

Cull the girls? That meant they killed them...right? Had her biological mother, or whoever had snuck her out of that herd, been caught? Had she gotten in trouble?

For as many questions as Dead of Winter answered, each answer raised three more questions.

"You okay?" Cheyenne asked from the bathroom doorway.

"Aaah!" Raven squelched out, shoving her tank top down to cover the scars. "I didn't hear you come in."

"I've been told I'm quiet for a human."

"No one in their right mind would ever call you quiet," Dead said from outside.

Raven laughed. Laughed. Her head was spinning with all this new information, but she was laughing.

Cheyenne sighed heavily and rolled her eyes to the ceiling. "She's fine, Dead. You can run along and fuck up the rest of your interview now."

"Nah," he said, barging into the bathroom. "I already put my three minutes in."

"You broke a chair, said four cuss words, shotgunned a beer on camera, and you called Rhonda a lily-headed-ninny-poof."

Dead leaned against the bathroom wall with a smirk. "I used my three minutes wisely."

Raven was having a giggle-fit because she could actually imagine him doing those things.

"Okay, well, I have to go introduce myself to my new client."

"Tell First Time Train Wreck to sleep with his eyes open," Dead growled.

"It's not his fault he won!" Cheyenne quipped. "Get our herd back together next event. Train Wreck is a jerk. I don't want to manage him. He's already texted me a list of snacks he wants in his changing room before events."

"We can do that?" Dead asked. "Add candy to mine. And cheese puffs." He pointed to Raven. "Any requests?"

"Uh, no? I won't be at the next event."

"Yes, you will." He turned to Cheyenne. "And dark chocolate squares. Bitches love chocolate."

"Dead!" Cheyenne gasped out. "You can't call women bitches!"

Raven was pursing her lips against a smile because Cheyenne was right.

"Fine. Heifers love chocolate. Better?"

Cheyenne parted her full lips but nothing came out. She looked confused. She shook her head, her dark hair twitching in its ponytail. "I'm not sure if it is or not."

She disappeared out of the bathroom and left Raven and Dead staring at each other.

"Sooooo," Raven drawled, "fancy meeting you here. In the bathroom."

"You were staring at your brand, weren't you?"

"No," she lied.

"I'm hungry."

"Me, too. I was too nervous to eat before I met you."

"Want me to feed you?"

"Uuuuh, feed me what?"

"It's late, and the only places open now will have

a lot of rodeo fans."

"That's a bad thing?"

"Not at all, but I will definitely get in a fight. Usually the team eats together after an event, but I messed all that up by accidentally breaking my friend, getting dropped a rank, and getting kicked off the team, yada yada yada."

"Well, then, there's only one thing we can do," she said. "Eat out of the dumpster out back like a couple of raccoons."

"I like that idea, but I have a better one."

"I'm all ears."

"We've been dating for a while now—"

"Oh, my God, again," she muttered.

"And I feel like it's time for you to see my mansion."

"Your mansion?" she repeated.

"Yep."

"I don't like boys with mansions."

"Rich boys aren't your type?"

"Nope. Not looking for a sugar daddy."

"Well, good thing for you I'm on a downward spiral of my career and probably won't be rich much longer. Enjoy my mansion while you can. I'll cook for you."

She crossed her arms over her chest and leaned back on the bathroom sink. "If you think you're going to take me to your fancy house and seduce me with a good meal, I don't hop into bed easy."

"Lucky for you, I'm not even trying to get you into bed." He opened the door and gestured for her to go first. "I'm a gentleman."

She made her way through and said over her shoulder, "I've caught you staring at my boobs, like, four times."

"Well, they're perfect, so maybe if you don't want me appreciating them, dress them up as saggy boobs for Halloween next year. The perky ones have my heart, and my heart is directly connected to my dick."

"That's sweet. I'm serious, Dead of Winter." Her voice died in her throat, and she had to take a couple steadying breaths before she finished. "I don't go to bed with men easy. That's not a challenge. That's me saying what I will and won't do."

He caught up and walked beside her toward a big, glowing orange exit sign. "Can you do me a favor?"

"Sure."

"Call me Dead. Dead of Winter is a name for the

fans. And I promise I'm not taking you to my place for that reason. Listen to my voice. You'll hear the truth there. I don't want to say goodbye yet, but I've stalled at this place as long as I can. They're gonna lock the damn doors on us."

She gave a shy smile at the ground and said, "You want to spend more time with me?"

"Yeah, raven girl with a big animal and a human life. You got my attention tonight. Plus, I need you to vent with me about how I was robbed of my rank."

"Totally robbed."

"Train Wreck is such a splinter."

"*Suuuuch* a splinter."

He chuckled and opened the exit door for her. A few cowboys were hanging around outside, and one of them told Dead, "You did good buckin' tonight, boy!" But the other two called him names and one of them said, "Now you're headed where you belong, Dead. To the bottom. Fuckin' bottom-feeder. Hey, lady, do you know what he is? An animal. Don't go home with animals. Have some pride in yourself."

Her stomach turned, and she clenched her hands at her sides to steady the animal that roiled in her middle. That's what riders thought of the bulls? "I guess I'm an animal too then, mister," she ground out.

Beside her, Dead was silent but, oh, his body shook, and power and anger vibrated straight from him to fill her lungs when she tried to drag in a breath. Raven had seen enough trash talk in her life to know they were just trying to get into his head. Dead probably dealt with that it all the time, but she didn't like it. Didn't like what it did to him or his bull either. A part of her wanted to change and let her animal have those assholes.

"Who was that?" she asked quietly as he led her toward an old lone truck parked under a streetlamp in the middle of a field the venue had turned into a parking lot.

"No one important," he said easy.

When he opened the passenger side door for her, she had to try three times to climb up into that jacked-up monster truck. On the third try, he placed his hands firmly on both of her butt cheeks and hoisted her into the seat.

She would've pretended to be offended, but she laughed and gave away her amusement.

"See?" he asked. "Gentleman."

Before she could respond, though, he said,

"Forgot something, but I'll be right back. Just stay here." His smile was a little too bright to go with his dark eyes.

He sauntered back toward the men lingering outside, his hands relaxed at his sides, swinging like he didn't have a care in the world, but she knew different. She'd felt his anger.

He made his way back to the cowboys, and in the shadows of the arena wall, she could make out a blur of moment.

Shoot! She shoved open the door and scrambled out, but that man didn't need any help. He was already headed back her way, a smirk on his lips and confidence in his gait. Oh, his knuckles were busted and bleeding, but he didn't favor them as he held the door, waiting for her to get back into his truck.

"Did you just beat them up?"

Dead shrugged. "They talked about you and made you mad. They won't make you mad anymore."

"Dead," she whispered, "you can't just beat up everyone who says something annoying."

"Why not?" he asked.

"Because..." Well, why not? "Because...oh heck, I don't know. It's against the rules or something."

"What rules are you living by, Raven? The human ones? Those don't count in cowboy country. They pop off, lookin' for a fight, and we give 'em a fight."

"But...what if they call the police?"

"I've had, like, five fights with those assholes. The police would just tell them to stop pissin' me off." After he shut the door beside her, she watched him stride around the front of the truck.

Dead was dangerous. If that much wasn't clear from the way he'd bucked and gone after that rider as an animal, it was clear as crystal with him fighting riders as a human. He wasn't even traumatized. He just wiped his bloody knuckles on his shirt and turned the engine over. It roared to life.

"Do you fight a lot?" she asked, her voice wrenched up higher than she'd intended.

"I don't know. What counts as a lot?"

"Once a week?"

"Oh, hell yeah," he said with a laugh. "Easy. Those riders can't keep their mouths shut. It's like they enjoy getting punched."

"Do they ever punch you back?"

"Yeah." When Dead turned toward her in the interior light of the truck, she could see it. His eye was swelling on his left side. "Don't go feeling sorry for them, Sugar Tits? This is part of the life."

"The life," she repeated softly.

"We don't call the cops or threaten to sue or throw a glass of wine in each other's face, Raven." He made a fist, and the cuts on his knuckles bled. "This is how we settle disputes. No one is allowed to talk to you like that. You understand? And if I ain't around? You better not be letting them talk to you like that either. You're a Hagan. You're a true black monster from birth, a longhorn shifter, and I would bet my boots you never sawed your horns down. What do you measure at?"

"Uhhh...that's personal."

"Fuck personal, be proud of your animal. I know you have the measurements. How big?"

She swallowed hard, but her answer still barely came out of her tightening vocal cords. "Ninety-six inches."

A slow, proud smile stretched his face. "Ninety-six. Inch. Horn spread. Never forget who you are, Raven. And don't let mouthy humans forget it either."

FIVE

"I like this way better than a mansion," Raven said as she stared at the huge camper sitting in an RV park just outside the arena.

"It's new. This is my first trip with it. Cheyenne has us flying to events, but this one was close enough to haul our campers to. Quickdraw's is over there." He pointed to a big black camper attached to a huge black truck. "And that one over there is Two Shot and Cheyenne's. They bought theirs when I bought mine. They seem to like it. It's better than hotels. I always feel trapped in a hotel."

"Because of the small space?" she asked, taking his offered hand as she climbed the three steps to the door he held open on his camper.

"Just too many humans. I feel like a sardine, crammed in with all them. I'm staying at Two Shot's ranch for a while, though, and Quickdraw had a camper, so I decided to look into them. Bought this last week and named him Big Daddy."

She giggled. "Perfect name. Ooooh, this is nice!" Inside to the right was a bedroom up a few stairs, and straight ahead, there was a small kitchen complete with granite countertops and a little stove and microwave and stainless-steel sink. To the left, there was a good-sized TV across from a leather couch, and even a little dining table. On the back wall of the camper was a bunkbed with mattresses and fancy comforters. This thing was nice!

"It's thirty-two feet long. Two feet bigger than Quickdraw's," he said with his lips twisted into a cocky smirk.

"Your knuckles are already healing," she pointed out as she looked at his hand resting on the edge of the dining table.

"Yeah, by morning there will be no evidence of a fight."

"Wow, I don't heal that fast!"

"I eat a lot of steaks."

Her eyes went so round they dried out almost instantly. "You eat cow?"

Dead waggled his eyebrows. "I can eat cow whenever you want."

She snickered and crossed her arms over her chest. "Okay, Mr. Famous Bull Shifter. What are you cooking me?"

"You aren't as shy as I thought."

Scrunching up her face, she said, "Being shy is annoying sometimes."

"Yeah, but you're fine in small groups. Just not in crowds. And who likes big crowds anyway? I don't."

"You're just being nice so I don't feel so bad," she murmured, dropping her gaze to the nice wood flooring. "This thing must've been very expensive."

"It's half paid off so my monthly payment isn't bad. I used my winnings from the last event on it. Figured it was a good investment."

"I'd say."

"Chicken."

"I'm not a chicken," she said.

"No, I mean I'm making you chicken tonight." He opened a fridge door and pulled out a package of chicken legs and a bag of zucchini.

"It's so crazy that you can cook in here," she murmured, in awe of what all this little home could do.

"Of course, but I'll probably never use that stove," he said, pointing to it with a pair of tongs. "I have a grill outside. Want to grab us a couple drinks? I'll go turn on the fire."

"Okay," she said and made her way to the fridge. She grabbed a couple of canned orange sodas and then washed her hands in the little kitchen sink. There were three sharp knifes attached to a strip of strong magnet on the wall above the sink, so she went to work, washing and cutting up the zucchini into spears.

"You don't have to do that," Dead said as he came back inside. "I'll cook for you. Go sit on down and relax."

"I like cooking. Plus, we're a pretty good team, as was super-evident from our work at the signing table tonight. I've never seen anything like that."

"Yeah, well, usually I fuck it up a little more thoroughly. I was showing off for you a little."

She laughed and set a few veggie spears into a glass bowl he pulled out from under the sink. "Do you always try to destroy everything?" she asked.

"Yep. It's in our nature."

"Not mine. I try to fix everything."

He didn't respond, so she turned to see if he'd grown busy, but he was just staring at her with this thoughtful look in his striking green eyes. "You're different."

"You mean weird. It's okay to say it. That's what I've heard my whole life."

"No, I said what I meant. You're different. In a good way. Interesting. Unexpected. Fun. You're like a puzzle where all the pieces fit just fine, but the picture is something different than was on the box."

She froze because her chest was doing something strange. It was fluttering, and her insides were turning, but it wasn't a bad feeling. "I...I think that's the nicest thing anyone has ever said to me."

"Mmm, well that's sad. I complimented your tits earlier, and you weren't nearly as grateful."

She laughed and poured olive oil over the veggies. "I respond better to the sweet stuff."

"Well, I read magazines on what women like, and from my extensive research—"

"Research?"

"From my extensive research, I have come to the conclusion that you like a man to be both a gentleman and a monster. You want a little spanking in the bedroom but for us to hold doors open. A little chokey-choke time during sex but then buy you flowers."

"Oh, you would never have to buy me flowers. I work with flowers all day long."

"You're a florist?"

"Kind of." She poured the lemon pepper seasoning he handed her onto the veggies. "I do flower arrangements for a few funeral homes. I work at a specialty shop that doesn't have customers come in or anything. It's just a warehouse type building where online orders come in from the funeral homes, and we bring the arrangements and set them up the day of the funerals."

"Wow. What made you want to work with something so morbid?" he asked quietly.

"For me, it's not morbid. I'm helping. These families go through great grief, and they're supposed to pick out flower arrangements on top of everything else they're dealing with. The funeral homes I work with try to streamline it and make it easier on the grieving families. They have our brochures there and put in the orders a couple of days before the events, My boss and I make sure those families have a seamless setup the morning of. I don't think it's a sad job. To me, it's fulfilling. I'm getting to help people when they are feeling at their lowest. Make their day just a tiny bit easier."

"Puzzle. Such a surprising puzzle."

She grinned. "Most people back away slowly when I tell them what I do for a living. Funerals are one thing people don't enjoy thinking about or talking about, but for me it's just a part of my work. A part of my day."

"So you're good at flower stuff. What else do you do for fun? Besides getting tattoos, stalking champion bull shifters—"

"Oh, I set my sights lower than that, Dead of Winter. I only go for third place bull shifters."

He chuckled. "I know I'm supposed to be offended, but I'm not. You came in at my lowest. I won't stay there for long. And call me Dead! I'm serious. It's weird hearing my whole name all the time. Spill your guts, woman. What do you do for fun?"

"Uuuuh...oh geez, I don't know. I haven't been asked this in a long time. Let's see, I like going to the King River with some of my friends on the weekends. I drink White Claws and trashcan punch, and I like jumping off cliffs into water. I went sky diving once. I'll try anything. I want to live while I can."

"Because you work for funeral homes?"

"Yes." She frowned and repeated, "Yes. How did you know?"

Dead shrugged and took pans of chicken wings he'd been seasoning and the veggies outside. "I just guessed. I bet you have a healthy respect for mortality."

"Yeah. Yeah, I do." Huh. For a big, gruff and tough man, he listened. Paid attention.

"Who are your friends?" he asked as she followed him out with their orange sodas. "More specifically, who is your wolf shifter friend, and is he hot?"

She snickered. "You jealous?"

"Well, we've been dating for a very long night, and I'm possessive," he murmured, opening the lid of his grill parked right at the corner of his camper on the gravel. "I want to know his name, height, how many fights he's been in, pack name, rank in his pack, address... You know, the basics."

"Mmm hmmm. Height, five-foot-four—"

"Oh, he's a shrimp shifter," he muttered.

Raven hid her smile and took a seat in one of the two lawn chairs near the grill. "Fight number, I don't know. Maybe three? Pack name, not applicable, lone wolf, and rank in the pack? I guess alpha."

"And his name?" Dead asked primly as he set the wings on the grill one by one with a pair of tongs.

"Annabelle."

Dead jerked his attention to her. "Wait, what? I thought wolves were all male."

"They're supposed to be." Raven shrugged and took a sip of her fizzy orange drink. He was still staring at her, so she braved-up and explained the bare minimum. Annabelle had secrets, but who would Dead tell? He was a shifter, too. He would understand. "Annabelle wasn't born a werewolf. She was made into one."

He shook his head, his eyes so round like the full moon behind him. "How old was she when she was turned?"

"Third grade, so she was eight. It was an accident. A wolf was out hunting and she was out playing in the yard. The wolf stopped himself from killing her, but he'd scraped her with his teeth, and she survived. I met her when I was in fifth grade. My parents actually tracked her down and befriended her parents. Moved us two states away so I could have a shifter friend. They didn't know much about shifters back then, but they figured out what I was real quick after they adopted me. And they wanted to keep me safe and keep my animal a secret, but they wanted me to have a friend. So, they rearranged their whole lives to give me Annabelle."

"And to give you to Annabelle," Dead said.

"Yes. The home I grew up in is right next to theirs. Neighbors, and both of our families protect each other. Like a team. Always have."

Dead grinned. "I'll say it again. You won."

"When you said that earlier, it took some weight off my shoulders I didn't realize I'd been carrying. One conversation with you, and I felt lighter. That's pretty cool."

"Well, that's what boyfriends do. We carry some of the weight."

Raven rolled her eyes at his obnoxious grin and rubbed the goosebumps on her arms.

"Cold?" he asked.

"Yeah, but I'm—"

Dead bolted up the stairs into the camper and was back with a hoodie in his hands before the door even had a chance to swing closed. Holy moly, he was fast.

"—tough," she finished her sentence.

"Stand up," he told her.

She set her drink down and stood. As he pulled the giant black hoodie over her head, she carefully shimmied her arms into the sleeves, and when she had the hem settled somewhere around the vicinity of her knees, he eased the hood off her head and smoothed out her mussed hair. His fingers turned to feathers as he tucked her hair behind her ears. She could feel the callouses on his strong hands when he cupped her cheeks and, for a moment, she thought he would kiss her. He hesitated, staring down into her eyes, and she wanted it. Dear God, she actually wanted a kiss from an almost-stranger, and she never did that. Never opened up fast or trusted a man with affection who hadn't earned it over time.

He didn't kiss her, though. He eased her back, grabbed her hand in his, and spun her slowly.

"What are you doing?" she asked with a smile.

Dead pulled her in, his one hand cradling hers, the other hand on her waist. "Just follow me."

He swayed to the side two steps, one back, two more steps, one back. She messed up. She stepped on his boots and stumbled and tensed up, gripped his hand so tight.

He smiled and pulled her to a stop. Took his cowboy hat off and put it on her. It was big but stayed in place well enough as she looked up at him.

He positioned his hand around hers again and whispered, "Don't think. Just melt."

And then his eyes capturing hers, he swayed them to the side two steps, back one. Two and then one. There was no music, but there didn't need to be. Dead had good rhythm.

She'd come here tonight to meet a stranger and ask him a question to try to cool a fire inside of her. But now she was slow dancing in the illumination of a few strands of outdoor lights hanging from a camper, dinner on the grill, and a good man taking her on her first two-step. And she knew he was a good man. Her inner animal hadn't been much help growing up, but she could see the good in people. She could hear the honesty of their voices and read the intentions on their faces.

Dead was a monster in the arena, but he was good outside of those rails.

He was good outside of those eight seconds.

On and on they danced, and he pulled her closer and closer until her cheek was resting right over his drumming heart. His hand was strong but tender around hers, and his other palm was pressed so comfortingly against the small of her back, holding her in place against him. They were so close that his hat shifted on her head, so he took it off and set it on the lawn chair, spun her again, and then went back to dancing without missing a beat.

He eased her back. "Just trust me." And then they really moved as he guided her in circles and figure eights all over that light-speckled gravel.

He'd called her a puzzle and then taught her how to dance. Tonight was one for the books. Probably the most illuminating night of her entire life in so many ways.

He guided her back to the chair, pulled the hat back over her head, and said, "I'm gonna make a cowgirl of you yet."

Her heart dropped, and she tucked her chin to her chest.

He lifted it with the curve of his finger. "You got sad. Why?"

"Because you and I know tonight is all we have."

"I don't know shit," he murmured through a crooked grin. "Ask Cheyenne."

"Halloooooo!" came a call through the night. Cheyenne and Two Shots Down were headed their way through the shadows that separated their camper from Dead's.

"We smelled chicken and you owe me sustenance," Two grumbled hoarsely. He was deeply limping on his left leg.

"Who says 'sustenance?'" Dead jabbed at him as he turned to check on the chicken legs. "I made enough for you moochers. Figured you would find your way here." He turned to Raven, and his eyes grew serious as he explained, "They are obsessed with me."

Two Shots Down offered a hand for a shake and introduced himself. "I'm Two Shots. Cheyenne told me about you."

"Hopefully it was good things," she said, ducking

her gaze as she shook his massive hand.

"Cow shifter, got Dead to sign through the entire line of his fans, ate half his bag of chewy sprees at the table, and he didn't even throw a tantrum. And you were nice to my lady." Two Shots winked and nodded. "You're just fine by me."

"Quickdick!" Dead yelled at the top of his lungs.

Raven and Cheyenne jumped like jackrabbits in startlement.

"Come out and eat while the eatin's good!" Dead yelled, flipping the wings on the grill.

"Did you just call him Quickdick?" Cheyenne whispered in horror.

"Yeah. I've been trying out new nicknames to call him during interviews. That one is my favorite. Second favorite nickname is for Two Shots."

"Oh yeah?" Cheyenne asked. "And what is that?"

"Two Shits."

Two Shots shoved him hard in the shoulder, and Raven had to clap her hand over her mouth to cover her laugh.

The creaking door of Quickdraw's camper opened slowly, filling the entire doorway with an angry giant. "What in the name of Satan's balls did you just call me?" he yelled.

"Oh, I must not have said it loud enough," Dead called out. "Let me try again." He sucked in air for a good yell, but Quickdraw beat him to it and screamed, "No!" The word echoed through the entire park.

Okay, now, Two Shot's shoulders were shaking with his quiet laughter.

The behemoth poured out of that little doorway and stomped down the stairs hard enough to rock the camper. His boots made little tufts of dirt clouds as he sauntered directly toward them and, oh God, "Are we going to die?" Raven whispered.

"Nah, just Dead'll be dead," Two Shots enlightened her as he pulled a couple of cold ones from a blue cooler sitting by the door of Dead's camper.

"Oh," she chirped. This orange soda wasn't nearly strong enough. Inside of her, the animal stirred. Uh oh. "Um, you should stop right there," she said in a soft, shaky voice to Quickdraw.

"What?" Quickdraw belted out.

Raven cleared her throat and shook her head apologetically, dared to look in his pissed-off, dark eyes. "You should be nice to him."

Dead leaned over and sniffed her. "You smell like fur. Smells good. Oh, my God, are you going to change?"

"I honestly don't know what to do with this," Quickdraw uttered, confusion furrowing his dark eyebrows. "She's little and quiet. I have to do what she says? Yes? Because she's a girl? Or...?"

"My girlfriend is a Hagan heifer, and she can kick your ass," Dead said through a grin.

Quickdraw's eyes went wide. "Really?"

"Well, I don't know about the kicking your ass part, but my animal kind of wants to give it a go."

"Nope. Nope, nope, nope, you keep her locked deep inside of you," Two Shots advised her. "We're all friends here, and friends don't let friends kill other friends."

Quickdraw looked at Cheyenne and back to Raven, then to Cheyenne again. He seemed highly offended now. "So, I can't even punch him?"

"I mean," Cheyenne drawled out. "...You can...but then you have to deal with Dead and the Bacon Heifer, whatever that means."

"Hagan Heifer," Two Shots corrected her. "Trusty trust me, we don't want her changing. My leg hurts like a sonofagun. Can we just eat and not fight? For freaking once? Huh? Can we just do that tonight?"

Quickdraw shoved Dead in the shoulder hard and jammed his finger in his face. "Don't call me that again."

Dead took a long drink of his soda and asked Cheyenne innocently, "How do you use hashtags on social media?"

"No!" Two Shots and Quickdraw yelled together.

Dead was grinning like a villain now, and Raven thought he was so handsome when he was being a little bit evil. She pulled her phone out of her back pocket and searched him up on Instagram, then followed Dead of Winter's page. And then before she could change her mind, she sent him a message.

Dear pretend-boyfriend,

It's our one-day anniversary, and that's a pretty big deal, so I figured it was time to give you my number.

She typed out the number and hit send, put her phone away, and settled onto the chair Dead pulled over to her, feeling an easing in her soul she'd never felt before.

Would she regret giving him her number tomorrow? Probably. She was an overthinker and would probably lie in bed tonight going over all the reasons she should leave him alone. They lived in different towns, probably different states, and she didn't have a lot of money to travel for a long-distance relationship or friendship, or whatever this would turn out to be. But she didn't get sad thinking about the end of the night anymore because there was this little connection out there in the universe between them. One that he didn't even know about yet.

Right now, it was her little secret that tonight wouldn't be the end of them.

SIX

"I'd better get going." Raven shifted her weight from side to side and hugged tight around her the giant hoodie Dead had given her.

Dead waved to his herd—that's what he'd called Two Shots Down, Cheyenne and Quickdraw—as they walked back to their campers.

"I was thinking you should stay here tonight," he said. "I got everything a girl could need to stay the night. I internet-searched a checklist of stuff chicks like, and I got a girlfriend starter pack all put together."

"A what?" she asked, controlling her smile. He looked very *very* serious here under the strands of outdoor lights.

"A girlfriend starter pack. Here, I'll show you. Oh," he said, turning before he opened the door. "And chicks like to know they're safe, so I promise I won't bone you unless you ask me to bone you."

Raven pursed her lips against a giggle that was threatening to bubble up the back of her throat. "Um, thank you for controlling your boning. I wasn't scared, though. You've been mostly a gentleman all night."

"I'm gonna need you to put that in writing and submit it to Cheyenne so she gets off my back. I'm basically contractually obligated to be a gentleman." He grinned brightly and pushed the camper door open and gestured her in grandly.

"What else does your contract say?" she asked curiously as she walked up the stairs and made her way into the camper.

"I'm not supposed to talk about it outside the herd." Dead pulled a blanket out of a cabinet. "You can sleep here, and I won't even make any mooooves on you. Cow joke."

She cracked up and plopped onto the couch where that rough-and-tumble man tucked her in like a little burrito with the blanket, which, by the way, smelled like his cologne and she was definitely going to try to steal it tomorrow.

There was a recliner by the tiny kitchen island, and he sat down there. Like a gentleman. "I'm supposed to be respectful during interviews—"

"I've seen your interviews. You've ignored that rule."

He laughed and nodded. "Yeah, you're right, rule ignored. I hate doing interviews. Wait! You watched interviews of me?"

Her cheeks heated again and she dropped her gaze, busied herself with pulling the blanket even tighter around her. "Um, I wanted to see what kind of person you were before I drove out here to meet you. I was curious about you. Not just because you were a bull shifter either. I mean...I was curious about what kind of man you were. I was scared you would see me in your VIP line and think I was just...I dunno...silly."

His smile slipped a little, and his green eyes churned with honesty. "I don't think you're silly at all. What did you learn from the interviews?"

"I learned that you're funny, and you don't care about impressing people. I liked that part. You're confident. The only time I saw you get serious was when an interviewer asked one of your herd a question they didn't like. You got protective of them. The humor would fade away from you face, and you would look…"

"Look what?" he asked softly.

"Terrifying."

"What else did you learn?" he asked low.

"I have a silly present."

His eyes went wide with shock. "You got me something?"

"It's nothing big. I was going to give it to you when I got to the front of your line, but I ended up working at your table instead and forgot it." She threw off the blanket and scrambled for her little purse she'd left by the door. The package of candy took up most of the space in the little satchel.

Raven took a deep breath before she turned around because she was nervous. Why? She had no idea.

"Happy one-night anniversary," she teased as she handed him the candy.

"Skittles?" he asked, taking the present from her.

"I saw you eating them in an interview once so I knew you liked them. But you were putting all the yellow ones back in the package so I know you don't like the yellows. I'll eat those if you don't want them."

He was staring down at the palm of his hand where the red Skittles package laid. "I take out the yellow ones for Cheyenne. They're her favorite color." He looked up at her and asked, "What's your favorite flavor?"

"Red."

"Mine, too."

She grinned big and sat back on the couch. Raven didn't know why, but she really liked that they enjoyed the same flavor. "Red ones taste the best."

"I got you a present, too," he blurted out. "But it was before I met you, so I didn't know what you liked."

Raven didn't understand, so she shook her head and said, "Wild boy, what did you get?"

"The girlfriend starter pack."

She brayed a laugh. "Okay, I want to see what's in it."

He stood and shoved the Skittles in his back pocket. As he passed her on the couch, he paused and leaned down, squeezed her knee and murmured, "Thank you. I don't remember the last time I got a present." And then he jogged up a set of narrow three stairs and into the bedroom, then reappeared a few seconds later with a cardboard box in his hands. He set it beside her on the couch and then took his seat again in the recliner.

She opened the lid flaps and immediately laughed. There was a half-empty bottle of hair-growth vitamins, a box of tampons, and a box of pads. "In case a girl needs to grow long hair or spontaneously starts her period?" she asked.

"Yep. I ate half those vitamins. They work, but the labeling freaked me out. It says for women, and I got scared I would grow titties or something, so I just added it to the starter pack. Those things are expensive, and I don't like to waste stuff. Periods are terrifying, but the list said sometimes you have them and you can't help what's happening to your bodies and that a woman would appreciate some understanding. Now...I don't understand none of that body business because y'all are as complicated as a spiderweb, but if you ever feel the need to talk about, educate me, or inform me about your periods, I will do my best to listen and not yawn or turn on music in the middle of that conversation. Now, look at the stuff underneath."

There was a gallon-sized Ziplock bag of chocolate bars. "Period snacks?" she guessed.

"Yup."

Under that were neatly folded light-blue sheets and a pillowcase.

"Chicks like clean sheets," he explained.

Touché to that, because she was in fact a chick, and she also in fact liked clean sheets.

Next was a pink makeup bag, complete with brand new foundation, mascara, eye liner, and a shimmery gold eye shadow, still in the packages. Next to that was an unopened trio of razors for sensitive skin and a travel-size shaving cream.

When she looked up to ask if it was for shaving her legs, he winked and nodded. "For your pussy. Girls like shaved pussies."

"Oh, geez," she muttered through her giggling.

There was a two-pack of toothbrushes, a travel-size toothpaste, three hair-bands, a really fancy brand of face wash, dry shampoo, a washrag, powder fresh deodorant, and a pair of pink lace panties, size medium, with the tag still attached.

"I didn't want to assume on the size so I have

bigger sizes if needed," he assured her.

Under all that was a shirt she recognized from the merchandise he sold at his table, a snack pack of cheddar crackers, some peanut butter pretzels, and a can of squeeze cheese.

"Chicks like snacks," he enlightened her.

And indeed, she did enjoy snacks. "Okay, everything about this is awesome. You will definitely impress every girl who comes in here."

Dead shrugged. "You're the first girl to see the starter pack."

"No way."

"Yes way. You're the very first," he said.

"But...you're so handsome. And strong. You have so many followers on your social media pages. And you have the best beard and a six-pack. And—and—you're famous!"

"I'm also picky as hell, but thank you for those compliments."

"I'm picky, too!" she blurted out. "I haven't dated anyone for two years."

"A prude. I like it."

"Ha!" She laughed too loud and clapped her hand over her mouth. Raven cleared her throat. "I'm not a prude."

"When was the last time you slept with a man?"

"My ex-boyfriend, three years ago," she rushed out so she wouldn't change her mind. She liked all this honesty. It was refreshing.

"He hurt you?"

She nodded.

"Burned you?" Dead asked quieter.

Another nod from her.

"Well, he didn't deserve you."

"How do you know?" she asked. "I'm a stranger to you. Maybe I'm awful."

"False. You like red Skittles, and you're shy but strong. You are nice and don't compete with women. Cheyenne is pretty, and you helped her instead of posting up against her. You lit up when you saw the clean sheets and squeeze cheese, so I think you like those. You're funny, but quiet-funny. Not the kind that needs all the attention on her. You like to be invisible by strangers but seen by people you care about. You're a hard worker and caring about people in their worst times. You overthink situations before you get into them. You like beer, but not as much as soft drinks. You're adventurous, but okay with spending nights at home. You are picky about the friends you make, but when you choose someone, you *choose* them and don't quit. You're empathetic and internally strong. You can see someone else's struggle and not only understand it, but make them feel better. You're thoughtful with gifts. You're quiet, but inside you are a monstrous badass that the humans in your life will never understand, or fully appreciate. You blush easy, compliment people easy, and you get along with people easy. You get pushed around to a point, but when a person reaches that point? Your animal will put them in their place. You understand the human and the shifter world. You're open-minded and resilient." He searched her eyes. "How close am I?"

"I think..." She swallowed hard. "I think you see me very well."

His crooked smile curved his lips just slightly. "It's late, and I would worry if you drove back home tonight. You should stay." He jerked his chin up the shallow flight of stairs to the master bed. "I would feel happy and like I'm taking care of you if you take my bed."

"But where would you sleep?"

He gestured with two fingers at the door. "There's a corral outside. I would rather go bull and know you're safe and warm in here."

"You can change for a whole night?" she asked. Her max was three hours as her longhorn.

"I can go for days. The more time I'm a bull, the better I feel."

She pulled out the oversize T-shirt from the girlfriend starter pack. It read *Dead, Dead, you're great in bed* across the tits. "You just want me to wear this."

"Guilty. I'll probably take a picture and put it on that stupid social media page Cheyenne started for me."

"That'll start rumors about who you're dating."

"Sounds good to me. Rumor: Dead is dating a hot-as-fuck purebred longhorn shifter with perfect tits and awesome tattoos. Yep, let's get those rumors started."

She snickered and shook her head. "You make me out to be way cooler than I actually am."

He shrugged and stretched his leg out toward her. "I think you're just fine."

She arched her eyebrow. "How the rumor should

really read: Dead is dating a purebred mess who doesn't know how to control her animal, who does crossword puzzles for fun, has four pet plants, a shyness problem, is fifty percent social anxiety disorder and fifty percent daydreamer, doesn't like change, and lives in fear of hurting people."

"Eeeeerk," Dead said, making a screeching sound. "Go back to the part where you're afraid to hurt people. What do you mean?"

"When I change into my cow? She's not friendly."

"Nowhere in any cow shifter handbook was it ever promised that a full-grown bovine was supposed to be polite. We're monsters, Raven. Who could teach a monster manners?"

"Me," she said stubbornly. "I want her to be nice."

"Because you're nice," Dead guessed. "I can tell you have a good soul. You care about people. Does it bother you that your animal didn't get those qualities?"

She nodded. "Very much."

"Well, the animal wasn't your choice. She's not yours to control."

"Yes, she is—"

"No, she isn't. Your animal is a part of you, but she

ain't you. My bull? You think I control him?"

"Yes?"

"Hell no. He tried to kill Cheyenne a couple weeks back just because she wore a red shirt. And because she's human. My bull hates two things. Humans and the color red. Guess what my favorite color is?"

"Red?"

"Red," he agreed. "Just to spite the hairy jerk that lives inside me. I don't get along with my animal. I bet if you ask Two Shots and Quickdraw, they don't resemble their animals either, and you know why? Because they're different critters sharing the same body. They aren't the same, Raven. Do you understand what I'm saying? You ain't your monster. You're just Raven with a bonus monster."

She giggled on accident. She'd been feeling so serious while listening and absorbing what he was saying, things clicking into place, but he'd called her inner moo "a bonus monster" with this little smirk on his face, and it had caught her off guard.

"I think you're very intelligent," she said.

"Well, don't tell anyone that. People go on thinking you're smart, they start asking questions geared for a smart person, and I'm not doing that shit.

Dumb questions only."

As Raven laughed, she propped her elbow on the arm of the comfortable couch and rested her cheek on her palm. "I don't think my animal hates humans. She's not picky. She just hates everything."

Dead's smile fell from his lips, and he relaxed back into his recliner, rocked it gently. "Mine can't stand humans. That right there is the real reason I rank at the top in this circuit. My bull can't wait to get a rider off his back. After he bucks, there's a few seconds that my animal lives for. The rider hits the dirt and then he's helpless, scrambling to his feet, slow. That's my bull's chance to get him. The bullfighters all know what I'll do at this point, know about the hatred, so they work tight and work well together to keep me off that downed rider."

"Have you ever hurt a human?"

"Oh, yeah. Every bull will hurt someone at some point. That's the part you have to accept. Two Shots killed a rider a few years ago. Now, I haven't had that kind of chance yet, but my bull would be happy if it happened."

"Would *you*?" she asked softly.

The look in his eyes was raw. "I would never be

okay again. And as much as my bull thinks that's what he wants, he would never be okay again either."

"Why does he hate humans so much?"

Dead smiled, clapped his hands on the arms of the chair, and stood. "It's late, and I'm sure you're getting tired."

There it was. That was a hard and unexpected shut down, and she instantly felt like she'd done something wrong. Said something unacceptable. "I'm sorry."

"Why'd you drop your eyes like that?" he asked.

Staring at the woodgrain pattern of the wood flooring, she shrugged up a shoulder. "Thank you so much for dinner and for spending time with me. And answering all my questions. I know it was a lot. I understand so much better now, though. I will be thinking about the things you said about my animal for days. I'm calling it." She forced a laugh. "I'll just get changed, okay?"

When she cast him a quick glance, he was standing there all tall-as-the-roof and strong, his hands on his hips and a frown furrowing his handsome face. "What's wrong with you?"

"Nothing."

He cocked his head and stared. She tried to hold his gaze. Truly, she tried, but she couldn't.

"Okay," he drawled out quietly. "You can use the bedroom to change. I'll be outside."

She swallowed hard and nodded, then took the entire girlfriend starter pack into the bedroom. The door clicked closed behind her and she sighed, but couldn't tell if it was from stress or from relief. The bed took up most of the room, but she had enough space to shimmy into the giant T-shirt. When she came out of the bedroom, she looked expectantly around the living area, but it was empty. He really had gone outside. A mix of disappointment and understanding churned in her chest. He was just being respectful. That, or he didn't want to be around her anymore. And that was okay! That was okay. Totally okay.

She made her way into the small bathroom where the sink actually worked. She brushed her teeth and pulled her hair into a messy bun and opened the door just in time for Dead to knock. He stepped back fast and shoved his hands in his pockets. "Sorry, I wasn't meaning to intrude. I just..."

"You what?" she asked.

He chewed on the corner of his lip and searched her eyes. "I made you uncomfortable, and I didn't like the way it made me feel. I wanted to find out why I made you uncomfortable so I don't make us feel like that again."

"You didn't make me uncomfortable, Dead. I just didn't want you to shut down. I wanted you to keep talking, telling me interesting stuff about yourself, and not go to bed yet. I know that's silly because you're a stranger and you've already opened up so much, but I guess I'm selfish and wanted more." She inhaled after saying all that on one breath. "I like learning about you."

The corner of his lips turned up in a smile for just a second before it disappeared. "You asked about why I hate humans."

She nodded and wrapped her arms around herself to hide her nipples perking up against the thin fabric of the T-shirt.

"I've never talked about that with anyone. It's a scary thing to do."

"Talking about personal stuff with a stranger?"

"Yeah."

"Well, you can look at it that way, or you could

91

see it as less risky. After tonight, you'll never see me again. And I'm good at keeping my word. I will never speak of your reasons again to another living soul. Not even my pet plants. So, you can share that story with someone who won't be affected in any way or judge you. And then you will have told someone. And maybe it won't be so scary to talk about it then."

"Filsa."

That word chilled her blood and made her skin tingle.

He backed up and sank into the couch. "I can tell by the look on your face you know what that drug does."

"It makes your animal go to sleep."

Dead rested one ankle on his knee and shook his boot slightly—a nervous tic, perhaps. "And how did you learn about Filsa?"

"My friend Anabelle has used it before. She wanted to see what it would feel like to be human again."

"Mmm." His eyes were darkening to the color of whiskey. "Only you aren't human when you have that drug in your system. You're still a shifter, just helpless to protect yourself."

92

"That's what Annabelle learned, too. Did...did you try the drug?"

"Not on purpose."

"Someone gave it to you?" Raven guessed, her stomach churning.

Dead's eyes glazed over as he looked at something faraway, something right through her. He nodded. "Someone did that."

"A human?"

Another nod.

"Who?" she asked.

His lips twisted up into a humorless, empty smile. "No one important anymore."

And it hit her. Hit her like a lightning strike and sent chills up her spine. "You never admitted your mother was a human before it was announced at your last rodeo. You never talked about her in interviews either."

Dead didn't move a single muscle.

So she took another guess. "Your mother gave you that drug?"

"She wanted a normal son. A human one. I changed for the first time at my seventh birthday party in front of all her friends. I'll never forget the look of mortification on her face. Or the sounds of her screaming and crying and asking the sky, 'Why me?'"

"Oh, my gosh." Raven closed the few steps between them and sank onto the couch beside him, tucked her legs right against his ribs and rested her head on his tensed shoulder. "How long did she give you the drug for?"

"I didn't even fuckin' know she was doing it for a year. Maybe longer. I just thought my animal had disappeared, but there was this anger left behind. I couldn't stop fighting the other kids in my class, and the more time that went on, the sicker I felt in the head. And, eventually, my body got sick, too. She wouldn't take me to the doctor. Said I was going through growing pains. Only my skin turned pale, and I couldn't keep any weight on, lost my appetite, was exhausted, my eyes were all sunken in. I looked like a corpse. An eight-year-old corpse. I thought I was dying. Hell, maybe I was.

"I'd never met my dad, but one day this big bear of a man kicked in our door. I was lying on the couch, staring at a television set that wasn't even turned on. He took one look at me, and I remember his eyes went so sad. Mom came barreling down the stairs with a shotgun in her hands, pumped it, and aimed it at his chest. She told him to get away from me, said he'd done enough. He told her to go ahead and shoot him. It's what it felt like when he found out I existed anyway, like he'd been shot. He accused her of giving me Filsa, and I didn't know what that meant. And, honestly, I didn't really care. I felt so awful I could barely lift myself off the couch cushion. I remember the rage in his eyes when he told her she'd ruined me. 'There ain't nothin' wrong with him, and you went and ruined him. You ruined him.' He told me to go pack a suitcase, but I didn't want to go with a stranger. I didn't know him. I shook my head, and I remember he picked me right up off that couch like I weighed nothing. He told me everything was going to be okay, and he carried me up the stairs, right past my mom, all folded up in his arms. He grabbed a duffle bag from my closet and emptied as many of my drawers as he could into it, then he grabbed the stuffed dog off my bed because I said I wanted it. My mom was hysterical in the hallway, said she was calling the cops, and he lost it. Told her to go ahead. They would take one look at me and know she'd been poisoning me. He told her if she ever contacted me again without my consent, he would burn the house down with her in it and make the world a better place for it. And I believed him. My dad has a dark place in his soul for humans that try to cut the animals from us. And it happened to his own son. He took me out of there and said all I needed was time. Explained what Filsa was. And then he pulled over at a gas station a few towns over, got me a gallon of water to start flushing my system and a package of Skittles."

Tears were burning her eyes, but she smiled at that and wrapped her arms around his middle, snuggled closer. "That's why you like Skittles?"

"He sends me a bag every time I buck. I get a care package of candy every week, along with a bunch of other random shit he finds at stores that remind him of me."

"How long did it take you to be able to change again?"

"About two days. The second that drug started wearing off, my bull came rampaging out of me. Dad had to camp out beside a corral for a couple weeks since I changed forty-fifty times a day. I don't remember much about the detox. Just that it hurt."

"Have you talked to your mom since?"

Dead shook his head. "Didn't ever get the urge to. My dad was good enough for me. I didn't yearn for my mom or feel like I was missing out. My bull, though? He never stopped thinking about her. Never stopped hating her. Now he takes it out on every human he can reach." Dead smiled brightly. "And that's the story about how fucked up I am."

"No, that's the story of a survivor. Look what you're doing?" she said, resting her legs over his. "You used something awful that happened to you to make a career. Look where you got to."

"A camper and a herd of misfits?"

She snorted. "No, silly. Number three bull shifter in the world. In the world, Dead. I don't even follow rodeo, and I know how big a deal that is. I saw the line of people waiting to meet you tonight. The signs that fans held up in the stands. The attention on your social media, the interviews, the time on television because everyone is curious about you. You." She poked him in the chest. "And not for the bad parts. You're funny and charismatic and caring in a surprising way. I think you did pretty dang good for yourself."

"You're a natural cheerleader, aren't you?" he

asked.

"Yep. Screw your mom and screw that poison. You lived. Not only did you live, but you got yourself from that corpse of a kid to this." She waved her hand at him. "With all the muscles."

He chuckled. "You like the muscles."

"I don't hate the muscles."

"You want to touch the muscles?"

She snickered and hugged his taut waist a little tighter. "I don't mind touching the muscles."

He held her closer. "This is kind of nice."

"Snuggling?" she asked.

"Spending a night with a stranger and feeling so comfortable."

"Because there's no risk! No hearts get involved, and tomorrow I'll just be some girl you talked to for a day at a rodeo one time. Some girl who worked your table and asked a lot of questions."

"Mmm," he rumbled. "Yeah, just some girl." But his voice sounded off. "And I'll be just a boy."

"No, a moo cow shifter," she joked.

"Bull shifter," he growled, tickling her ribs suddenly.

Raven squealed and kicked her legs, tried to

tickle him back but he'd grabbed her wrists.

She froze, and he froze, and there they sat, faces inches away from each other, her arms held, completely vulnerable as he searched her eyes. His had lightened to a vibrant green.

She was panting, wanting, terrified and excited and happy and hopeful all at once.

He leaned forward suddenly and pressed his lips to hers. One second, and it was done. He eased back in a rush and released her wrists from his iron grasp. One second was all it took for her lips to throb, her cheeks to heat, and her body to move closer on its own accord.

"I'm sorry," he whispered, but he stayed just inches away from her.

"No, you're not," she whispered back. And before he could say anything, she leaned forward and gently settled her lips on his. His mouth softened, and he pulled her legs more securely onto his lap. Then with his other hand, he cupped her neck.

She'd never felt more safe, more secure, than in this moment.

His lips plucked at hers, moved with hers and, God, he tasted good. His beard tickled her, but she got used to it fast. Touching it with her fingertips helped, and when she did, he moaned softly into her mouth and leaned into her more. Masculine, dominant man. His kiss stayed easy for a long time. Minutes? Hours? She didn't know. She hadn't a guess because time meant nothing in his arms. But the longer she was with him, the more his warmth seeped into her skin and she melted into him.

His lips left hers to kiss her cheek, down her jawline, her neck where he stayed, paying attention to her sensitive skin right over her tripping pulse. Wrapping her arms around his neck, she leaned her head back to give him more room to tease.

With a soft grunt, he gripped her hips and pulled her onto his lap, her legs straddling his hips. The size of his erection was intimidating, but oh so sexy all pressed against her, only separated from her by their clothes. Dead went back to kissing her neck, nipping, playfully biting. His tongue felt so good as it flicked out and touched her earlobe. He ran his hands slowly down her back, from her shoulder blades to her hips, and then cupped her ass. She rocked toward him.

Big hands. Strong hands.

"You like that?" he asked, squeezing her ass

gently.

She eased back and nodded. Why did she feel so drunk right now? Or high? On life? He was doing something to her body. Intoxicating it with his touch, perhaps.

She liked his effect on her. It was terrifying to let a man have so much control, but maybe she was ready to be scared in such a way. It had been a long time since a man touched her, and never like this. Never like he was coveting her.

This connection he was building between them felt important.

Feeling brave, she rocked her hips against his. He gripped her waist on a groan, his fingers digging into her skin. With a smile, she tugged at the hem of his T-shirt until he lifted his arms up and allowed her to peel the fabric off him. His chiseled six-pack flexed with his breath, and his hair was all mussed, his smile lopsided. God, he was beautiful, if that word made any sense about a big, powerful man like him. A tattoo encircled his pec and shoulder. Tribal symbols followed the curves of his muscles. He didn't take his eyes off her while she traced some of the lines of ink.

And he had this look on his face...

"What?" she asked, glancing at him, then away. At him. And away again.

"You're beautiful."

Her smile stretched her whole face. She busied herself with tracing the tattoo and then the curve of his shoulder down his triceps. "I am?"

He rubbed his thumb over the tattoo of the ram on her upper thigh. "I've never seen anyone like you."

"Oh, I'm nothing special," she whispered.

He lifted her chin with the tip of his finger and then cupped her cheek. "You're so wrong about yourself." Dead dragged his touch across her collarbone and then down between her breasts.

She was heaving breath by the time he reached her stomach. Just under the hem of her sleep shirt, he touched her skin, and she did something that shocked her. Something she'd never done before. Raven leaned forward and hugged him. Just wrapped her arms around his neck and rested her cheek against his. And he hugged her right back. Dead didn't hesitate. He wrapped his arms around her middle tight and held her close, their heartbeats drumming against each other.

"This is what we should do tonight," he

murmured against her ear as he rocked her back and forth gently.

"What?"

"Just keep it here. Not push it farther."

She waited a few seconds to respond because it took a little bit to process the disappointment swirling around in her chest. "You don't want more?"

"I've never wanted anything more than to flip you over on this couch and yank your panties off and bury myself inside you, Raven. I want you screaming my name. I want you coming over and over. I want to feel you gripping my dick while you beg to come again." He eased back and looked her in the eyes. "But you ain't a one-night-stand kind of girl. You're bigger than that. Better. I can't push us too fast and feel good about it tomorrow."

She nodded, pretending to understand. Why did she feel so rejected right now? Her hormones were going crazy, wanting more. He'd made her wet, made her yearn for him, and then backed off. Even though it was for an honorable reason, her body was being a little ho right now.

"I understand."

"Good. So, I'm gonna need you to call into work

for the next week and come on the road with me so I can get more time with you."

"What?" she blurted out.

"I'm not interested in a one-night stand, but I would definitely stick you with a dick on a second date."

"Oh, my gosh," she said through her shocked laughter. "I can't... I can't just call into work."

"Why not? You don't have any vacation days left?"

"Well..." She actually hadn't taken any time off in two years. Her boss had actually been telling her she needed to get a life. "I don't have any clothes."

"Well, we have options there. You can wear all the Dead of Winter merchandise you want, or we can go shopping. I'll choose your lingerie if you get stuck and can't decide."

She was stunned, just sitting here straddling Dead of motherfreaking Winter's lap while he asked her to spend a week with him.

"Like a road trip?" she asked.

"We're going to Lubbock next, down in Texas. It's about twenty-four hours of driving and we have five days to get there, so we can set up for the rodeo down there. We'll have to stop along the way so me and the boys can train, but Cheyenne has all that worked out. She's found bucking chutes along the way. She's basically connecting the dots on a map with training until we reach Lubbock. And if you need to change, we can give you space in an arena to let your animal out. Safely."

"I...I don't know. I've never done anything like this."

"Then it's the perfect time to do it. Live a little. I won't let anything happen to you. I'll buy your flight back home when you have to go back to work. Come see my life. Spend time with bull shifters and learn about yourself this week, too. I'll get you a front row seat at the rodeo, right near the chutes. And then I'll let you work my signing table in Lubbock."

She giggled. "Putting me to work."

"Nah," he told her softly, "I liked tonight. You're a good teammate. You smiled a lot. It was fun to watch you with the fans. That was the first time it's ever been fun for me, and it was because you were there. I'm not ready to say goodbye yet."

With a shaky sigh, Raven told him, "I can message my boss, but she's probably asleep by now. And if she says no, I'll have to leave early in the morning so I can get to work on time."

"If she says no, I'll take you to work. Make sure you get there okay. But do me a favor and at least try? This long drive will be way more fun with you riding shotgun and giving me hand jobs."

She laughed because he was tickling her again. When he stopped, she went limp and plopped onto the couch beside him. "Fine, I'll try. She'll probably say no because it's short notice, but at least I can say I tried to have an adventure with you."

With Dead of Winter. The third-ranked bull in the world! And he wanted to spend more time with her? Her? The misfit, human-raised, shy-as-hell cow shifter? And he was looking at her like she was gorgeous? Like he was the lucky one? She'd obviously fallen into some portal and ended up in an alternate dimension or something.

She pulled her phone out of her purse and yelped at the number of missed calls and text messages from Annabelle and her parents that popped up on the screen. She texted, *I'm okay! Had a great night and still hanging out at the rodeo!* into a group text with her parents and Annabelle to keep it all simple. Then she messaged her boss about taking a week off, knowing it was much too short-a notice to actually work. But here with Dead, it was kind of fun to hope, to imagine how a week traveling across America with him would be.

The second she dropped her phone back into her purse, Dead picked her up and tossed her over his shoulder. And then that brute of a man smacked her right on the ass hard enough to sting, but in a good way. He took her straight up the three stairs to the bedroom and settled her onto his bed.

"You changed your mind about a one-night stand?" she guessed.

"Nope. I'm gonna respect the shit out of you."

When Raven pouted out her lower lip, he laughed and poked her lip back in with his fingertip. "No puppy-dog eyes. I'm a sucker for those."

Raven sat with her legs crossed and straightened her spine, made her eyes really big and blinked slowly. She was pretty good at puppy-dog eyes.

"Mmmmm," he ground out, his arms on either side of her hips. He rocked forward and kissed her.

Tempting him, she scratched her nails gently up his bare stomach, and he emitted a low rumbling sound that drew chills up her forearms. Holy hell, he was so sexy.

She ran her hands through his messy hair, smoothing it out of his eyes so she could see him better.

His expression went all serious. "I'm supposed to cut my hair and trim my beard."

"Why?"

"It's in the contract. I guess to look more clean-cut."

Raven canted her head and smoothed his hair back. "I can see your eyes better this way."

A slight smile lifted his lips and then fell. "You would like it?"

Silly Dead. "I would like the way you look any way."

"I can hear the truth in your voice."

"Cow shifters never lie," she said, trying to control a laugh.

"Bullshit. All them bull shifters in that rodeo tonight are liars."

She giggled and laid back on his bed. "I said cow shifters, not bulls. You boys are terrible."

"Agreed." He pulled the covers up and tucked her in like a burrito.

"Wait, will you sleep in the camper? Instead of out in the corral?" she asked as he stood and flicked off the bedroom light.

Dead leaned on the open doorway, all doused in shadows with the living room light behind him. Shadows and highlights accented his chiseled jaw, the curves of his arms, his abs. Handsome man. "I'll sleep on one of the bunk beds."

"Gentleman."

His smile turned crooked. So, sooo handsome. "Don't tell anyone, though. I have a horrid reputation to uphold."

She zipped her lips. "Your secrets are safe with me." She hugged a pillow to her stomach and turned serious. "All of your secrets are safe."

His eyes were so soft, so steady on her. "Goodnight, Raven."

"Sleep like the dead, Dead."

SEVEN

Sleep like the dead, Dead.

"You embarrassed me in front of all of those people!" Mom shouted.

A whimper escaped him, and he drew his little knees to his chest as he cowered in the corner.

"I knew your daddy was a monster, but I didn't know he was like those—those—shifters! And now he put that monster in you, and what am I supposed to do? Huh? I didn't sign up for this!"

"I can say I'm sorry to them," he squeaked out. "I didn't mean to." I'm scared. That hurt. There is a bull inside of me, and now I can feel him. I'm scared! I'm

scared!

"You know what? Don't even bother. They won't want to be friends with me after this. I have a freak for a son. Who would want to be involved with what's going on?" Her hair was tight in a ponytail this morning, and it made her bright green eyes look even meaner. *"Huh? Answer me. Who would want to do this with us?"*

"I don't—"

"Answer me!"

"I don't understand," he wheezed out. I'm so scared. And the bull inside of me feels like he's getting big again.

"Want me to kill her?" a voice rumbled through his head. He shook his head hard and whimpered. I'm scared.

Mom sighed and rested her hands on her hips, shook her head. "I'm going to fix this for you because that's what good mommas do. They fix their children."

Fix me?

"I've already contacted people who can help us. You're going to be normal again. Don't worry. I'll make it all right. My baby boy is dead right now, but I'm going to get you back."

He was dead? He looked out the window at the falling snow, and nothing made sense anymore. Nothing. It was so cold. Deep winter. He was dead? I'm scared.

"Momma has to go meet with someone for a little while, and it's best you stay here. Don't want to risk taking you in public if that thing will come out of you again. I'm going to meet with someone very important. Someone like you who will teach me how to fix you."

The animal was getting too big. He hated Mom. His blood was boiling with a mixture of rage and fear. Pain blasted through his head, and he whispered out, "Momma, help," as he doubled over in agony. It happened so fast, and then he was on four legs. And then he was standing, head down, heart filled with something dark that made his whole body hurt.

Momma screamed, "You're an abomination!" She moved to close the door. She would lock him in here.

And then the young bull charged.

Dead sat up with a gasp and hit his head on the bunk bed above him. "Mother...freaking...son of a Pegasus. Ballsack." He rubbed the knot on the top of his head.

That was his least favorite dream-memory ever. It was the birth of his bucking name. *Thanks, Ma.*

Warmth trickled down his eyebrow, and he squeezed his eyes closed so blood wouldn't get inside. Dead shoved off the bed and made his way to the bathroom in the dark. The cut had already slowed it's bleeding by the time he wiped it off with a folded wet tissue. He locked his arms against the sink and stared at himself. He looked haunted right now.

This was the time he always went to the bar. The only cure he'd found for the memories was a in a bottle of whiskey. His keys were by the door.

In the bedroom, Raven sighed in her sleep, and he turned his ear toward the sound. He didn't want to wake her up, but just that little noise that said he wasn't alone eased the tightness in his chest.

He didn't really want to go to a bar. They would close in an hour, and he felt anchored here. He didn't want to leave Raven.

But pieces of that memory and a hundred others were flashing behind his eyes, and he couldn't just keep glitching. Glitching meant the bull would come out of him ready to fight.

Maybe the tense feeling behind his sternum

would feel even better if he saw Raven.

Quietly, he made his way up the stairs, careful to avoid the creaky one, and stood in the doorway. His night vision was excellent, and thank the Lord for the blessings of the beast inside him, because Raven looked so pretty all curled on her side, hugging a pillow, her full lips slightly parted, a little worried furrow drawing her dark eyebrows down. Pretty girl. He liked when she wore his T-shirt. A sense of possessiveness nearly overwhelmed him. He should get her more T-shirts. Maybe one's he'd worn so she could smell like him.

He'd forgotten to turn off the strands of outdoor lights, and the soft glow was filtering in through the open blinds, casting her cheeks in warm lighting. Pretty, pretty Raven. A bird of a human with a monster of a longhorn inside of her. What a unique woman. He hadn't been lying when he'd told her he'd never met anyone like her. Everything about her drew him to her and made him want to learn more.

Momma has to go meet with someone for a little while, and it's best you stay here. Don't want to risk taking you in public if that thing will come out of you again.

He made his way to the door, but for the life of him, he couldn't pull the door open. He stood there frozen, caught between the memories and the woman in the other room. He wanted to go drink himself numb or turn into his bull, just to dull the remnants of that dream, but he didn't want to leave Raven.

Maybe he had whiskey here. Two Shots had brought some over the other day. He walked into the kitchen and pulled open the corner cabinet, and there it sat—a bottle of Jameson.

But he couldn't reach for it. He froze again as Raven sighed in the other room.

Was she dreaming, too?

Selfish creature that he was, he tiptoed into the bedroom for a fix he had never tried before. He hesitated by the bed, but his chest did feel better, and his head felt clearer. His mother's voice was just a whisper now, and whispers, he could deal with.

He pulled up the covers and slipped into bed behind her, wrapped his arms around her, and pulled her back against his chest.

And all his tension went away as if it had never existed at all.

EIGHT

Raven curled back into him, stretching her legs against his. "Dead?" she murmured sleepily.

"Go back to sleep. Everything is okay."

His voice sounded thick, though, so she twisted around and studied the grim line of his lips in the soft glow from the window. "What's wrong?"

"Just a dream. I wanted to sleep in here if you're okay with it."

"Of course, I am." She faced him fully and then massaged the back of his neck to his shoulders. "If you say a dream out loud, it won't come true."

"It already came true."

"Oooh," she murmured. She ran her nails down his arm, then to his back. He rolled his eyes closed and moaned.

"I have a theory," Raven uttered softly.

"About what?"

"About why you're so funny and feed off of making people laugh."

He cracked a smile, his eyes still closed against her scratching his back. "So, you think I'm funny."

"Hilarious. But sometimes the people who smile the most are the ones who have taken on the most damage. Jokes are your camouflage."

When he opened his eyes, they were the dark brown of his bull's. "You're terrifying."

"Because I'm right?"

"Because you look too closely and see too much."

She leaned forward and pecked his lips, then eased back again. "I feel the same about you, so we're even."

And then he told her a story about how his bucking name came to be—Dead of Winter. The words tumbled from his lips in the dark like a waterfall. He told her about the day after his birthday party, how his mother had gone to meet a drug dealer who was a shifter. That night would be the first time she slipped Filsa into his meal. He hadn't understood what was happening at the time because he'd been a scared kid, but he'd put everything together with his dad later. She'd told him her boy was dead. Her ramblings went on and on, insults falling from her lips like the snowflakes fell from the clouds outside. That snowstorm was one that was burned into his head. Dead of Winter had been named. Only he didn't choose it until years later when that memory visited his dreams every night for months. It was a way of owning his past. He told her he'd never shared the origin of his name with anyone but his dad, and her heart both hurt and soared for him.

Sharing burdens could be freedom, but often people didn't learn that until their troubles had eaten away at them. And for a strong, independent, intelligent, tough-as-nails bull shifter like Dead? She would bet her pet plants that he'd let them eat away at him instead of burdening anyone else with the truth of how he came to be.

For her, though? She'd met a stranger, and the things he'd revealed allowed her to fall in love in one day. She knew she was falling. She could feel it down to her soul.

It wasn't love at first sight. It was love at first

share.

When he grew quiet, she snuggled closer to him and rested her cheek on his chest. His heart was beating so hard—bum-bum, bum-bum, bum-bum. Up and down his back, she gently ran her nails until his heart stopped racing and his breathing steadied out.

"I love your name," she whispered. "It's a stronger name than anyone even realizes."

Dead laid a kiss on top of her head and hugged her tighter. "Sleep now, pretty Raven. You're safe."

And just before she slipped into sleep again, she murmured, "So are you."

NINE

"So then I asked her to travel with me this week and see what my job is like."

Raven sat up in bed with a grumpy frown. Dead was talking to someone in the living room. A glance at the clock, and she wanted to groan and pull the pillow back over her head. It was five in the morning.

"And what did she say?" Raven's dad asked over the speaker phone.

What the hell? She bolted out of bed and stumbled down the stairs to find Dead, fully dressed, his hair wet from a shower and a bright grin on his face Facetiming her parents while he sat in the recliner.

"Mom?" she asked. "Dad?" They were both

crammed into the tiny screen of Dead's cell phone. "How did you get Dead's number?"

"Your hair looks a little wild, honey. Maybe fix it a little so you can keep this boy impressed," Mom said, right before she took a sip of coffee from the *#1 Mom* mug Raven had made her in fifth grade. "Dead called us to have a coffee date and introduce himself."

"Okay, stalker," she muttered, patting her hair into place as she sat on the arm of his recliner.

"Actually, your dad called your phone three times, and I didn't mean to be nosy, but it was lighting up. I used his number from your phone and called him off my phone to make sure everything was okay. And also to introduce myself. Meeting the parents is a big deal. Also, your boss texted that you can have the week off. I didn't mean to see that either. It came through when I was looking for your dad's number."

Excitement rattled through her. "Really? I'm off for a week?" She bolted to her purse and pulled out her phone and, yep, her boss had really agreed. *About time you had some fun. Just come back next Tuesday. I can have Zeke fill in for you until then. He's been looking for extra hours anyway.*

"It's so great that you finally have a boyfriend!"

121

Mom said through Dead's phone in her cute little high-pitched voice. But then she lowered her voice and her eyes grew so earnest. "And he's like you. He's a *shifter*."

"Why did you whisper that last part, Mom?" Raven asked, taking a seat on the arm of Dead's chair again. "He knows he's a shifter. It's not a secret."

"Well, Marian, we better let these two get ready for their trip," Dad said, adjusting his glasses. "Dead, it was sure nice to finally meet you."

"Finally?" she asked.

Dead shrugged and grinned even bigger. Okay, she had to admit, he was very *very* handsome in the mornings with his wet hair all slicked back. He smelled so good, like bodywash. He was definitely a morning person. She on the other hand? Not so much.

"Okay, we love you, honey!" Mom called, waving. "Call us soon. Send us pictures of the places you see!"

"Bye, Baby Cow," Dad said low. "Dead, it was a pleasure."

"Same, sir. It's really good to meet y'all."

And before Dad could hang up, Mom was already talking about, "Oh, Dan, he's such a nice man and sure seems to adore our Raven and—"

Raven's cheeks were two hot flames right now, so she pressed her cool fingertips against them to try to ease the blush. "You met my parents."

"They're awesome. They assumed we've been together for a while. I didn't know how to correct them so I rolled with it. Did you know it's your mom's birthday next week? We should send her something."

"Okay," she uttered, shocked.

Dead wrapped his hand around her waist and squeezed her butt. "You look good in the mornings."

Raven glanced down at her giant T-shirt that made her look like a sack of potatoes and tried to pat her hair down again, but it was a very stubborn bird's nest right now. "I thought all shifters had good eyesight," she teased. "You're clearly blind."

"Girl, I'll bend you over right now, prove I like you just fine the way you look first thing in the morning. Feel." He pulled her hand onto his lap and, yep, there was his thick erection. Whoa, he was intimidatingly big.

"You had a boner while my parents were on Facetime with us?" she asked.

"Boners are natural and, besides, it's not my fault. You're the one who came in here bouncing them bra-less titties and looking all sexy with your bed hair, your purple fingernails, your matching toenails and, ooooweee, did you shave your legs yesterday?" he asked, running his hand up her smooth thigh.

She laughed because it tickled. "Maybe."

"Ooooh girl, I'm gonna get you in some cowgirl boots, and then good luck keeping me off you."

She dropped her gaze and fidgeted with a loose string on her shirt. "Maybe I don't want to keep you off me."

He growled through a wicked little grin and pulled her onto his lap. "Wish granted. Leaning into her, he sucked hard on her neck.

"Dead, you little turd, you're going to make a hickey!"

"Good. Then everyone will know you're taken."

It was raining this morning, and the patter of rain on the roof of the camper soothed her. She relaxed into the moment and slid her arms around his neck, arched her chin up slightly so he could reach his workspace. "You're a good sucker."

"That's what she said," he murmured against her throat.

"That's what who said? We've been dating a day,

and I'm territorial."

"Speaking of," he murmured, easing back from the definite hickey he'd made. "I got on my Instagram account this morning to post some pictures of last night, and someone named mayhillfuneralflowers sent me a message. She gave me her number. Now, I looked at her page, and she doesn't have any pictures of herself, so I couldn't tell how hot she was. It's just a bunch of pictures of flower arrangements. But my little heart started pumpin' faster, hopin' it was from you."

"Mmm, what pictures were you going to post?"

Dead picked up his phone from the arm of the chair and poked some buttons, and in her hand, her phone started ringing. He showed her the screen of his phone where he'd entered her name as *Wifey*.

She brayed a laugh. "There's so many red flags with you."

"Okay, but let's make them blue flags because my bull hates red."

"Dead, Dead, he hates red."

"Your hickey is red, and I kind of like that."

"Oh, my gosh," she murmured, pushing off him to look at it in the bathroom mirror. He did fast work. It was already a deep red bruise. Impressive, since it hadn't hurt, only felt really, really good.

"Save my number, woman," Dead said from the other room. "I just posted!"

"What?" she asked, slathering toothpaste on her toothbrush.

"I posted on my social media. Cheyenne will be so proud."

She finished brushing her teeth and made her way to the living area to find Dead holding a pair of scissors, cutting up a T-shirt on the small kitchen table.

Curious, she asked, "Do you do arts and crafts every morning?"

With a sexy arch of his dirty-blond eyebrow, he lifted the small shirt into the air. It was a black and white Battle of the Bulls T he'd cut into a tank top.

"For me?" she asked.

He nodded. "Yup. And I even made little rips in it with a box cutter."

"That's my style!" she exclaimed, running in place. "You made me a shirt!"

He chuckled. "Technically, I stole it from Cheyenne's inventory in the back seat of her truck this morning, along with two more shirts, a lanyard, and a sticker of my face." He held it up, and it was, indeed, a die-cut sticker of him making a silly face. "You may place it on your nethers."

She giggled and took the shirt from him, studied it. Okay, the man knew how to cut up a T-shirt. That, in itself, was a skill. "Is there anything you can't do?"

"No, I'm great at everything. Now, go get changed. It's raining."

She frowned out the window and then back to him. "So we need to leave earlier because the roads will be wet?" she guessed.

"Nope. Quickdraw probably isn't even awake yet. Just go get dressed. I've got something better than coffee that'll wake you up."

There was mischief in that man's eyes that had her heart rate thumping a little faster. What was he up to?

She brushed out her hair and put it in a ponytail, then shimmied into her shorts and the shirt Dead had made for her. Her black lace bra was showing a little through the rips he'd cut, but that was okay. She really loved this shirt! And it meant a lot to her that he had made it into her style, not into his. After she pulled on her boots and put on a layer of makeup from the girlfriend starter pack, she walked out into the living area of the camper and strutted around like she was on a catwalk.

Dead whistled and stared and made her feel like a million bucks with his compliments.

A good man knew how to hype up his lady. Even though she wasn't his lady. Not really. They'd just met. Yeah.

He pushed open the door of the camper, and they ran to his jacked-up truck.

"I drive a Prius!" she called as rain pelted against her hair.

"One of them clown cars?" he called, unhitching his truck from the RV.

"It's not that small. Plus, I get a million miles to the gallon."

"But how do you haul anything? Or make beer runs? Or run over people who annoy you?"

Her face must've been horrified because he looked up through the pouring rain with a grin and said, "Just kidding...probably." He cranked something on the hitch. "Get on in. This will only take me a second."

Raven scrambled into the cab of his truck and looked around. There was another cowboy hat sitting on the dashboard and a small duffle bag of worn ropes. Maybe to train with? She pulled one out and sniffed. Smelled like Dead, but not human Dead. It was a mixture of Dead and fur. She loved it and committed the scent to memory.

At the next row of RV's, Cheyenne was at the door of her and Two Shots' camper, yelling something.

Raven rolled down the window to hear better.

"No, Dead," she was saying. "If you tear up that field, I have to deal with the venue. I made pancakes! Dead! Are you listening?" Cheyenne was still wearing red plaid pajama pants and a red tank top, no bra. Pretty lady! "I wanted to have a herd breakfast before we go!"

Quickdraw opened his camper door and glared at Cheyenne. "What kind of syrup?" he called across the way.

"Why are you naked?" Cheyenne demanded of the tattooed behemoth who was, in fact, as naked as the day he was born.

"We're going muddin'," Dead yelled through the rain. "Want to go?"

Quickdraw flipped him off and disappeared into his camper, the door swinging loudly closed behind him. Dead didn't seem to mind and scrambled into the driver's seat, humming something to himself.

"He's a little rude," Raven whispered.

"You'll get used to him." Dead gestured to Quickdraw's camper, and the beastly man had appeared again with a pair of jeans on and nothing else save a set of keys dangling from his fingers as he jogged toward his truck.

Dead turned on the engine, and the dang thing roared like a hurricane. He revved it a couple times and then honked. "Two Shots, don't be a pussy! Let's go!"

Cheyenne was looking mighty enraged as she stood there, legs splayed in their doorway, her arms crossed over her chest. "No!" she yelled as Two Shots tackled her from behind, folded her into his arms with the keys dangling from his grinning mouth. He gave Raven a wink as his mate flailed in his arms.

"I always have to pay for the damage you boys do!" Cheyenne yelled. "Rule number eight! No damaging venue property!"

"It's just a little dirt, Cheyenne," Dead called out

Raven's open window. "You can't hurt dirt." He cast a crazy smile at Raven and hit the gas. The truck peeled out and threw mud and gravel behind the tires.

"Might want to roll that window up unless you want a mud bath," he told her over the roaring of the engine.

"What are we doing?" she called, rolling it up as fast as she could.

"Muddin', woman!" He twisted and checked the bed of his truck. "Last time I did this, I had my camp chairs and a bag of clothes in the back and caked them. Learned my lesson."

Eyes wide and arms locked against the dashboard in fear, she tossed a look in the bed on instinct. "Dead, there's still camp chairs and a bag back there!"

"Okay, maybe I didn't learn my lesson." He hit the gas, blazing between two rows of RVs. In the side mirror, she could see Quickdraw's giant-ass truck following right behind them, and when they hit a curve, she could see Two Shot's white truck behind him.

People were sticking their heads out of their RV doors as their trucks blasted by. Mostly cowboys lookin' either grumpy-as-hell or curious. Raven didn't

131

know what else to do other than wave apologetically. *Sorry for waking you up with three loud trucks and chaos.*

He hit the end of the RV camp and aimed for the tree line that bordered the huge clearing.

"Oh, my gosh, Dead! I don't think we're supposed to go in there!" The trees were too tightly grouped. They were going to crash! She threw her arms over her face. "Dead, slow down!"

"Raven," he said, aiming for an opening between two trees. "I won't let anything happen to you. Just live!"

Just live.

When she peeked from behind her arms, they were already through the trees. In this stretch of woods, the foliage wasn't so compact, and Dead skidded around a patch of brambles and hit the gas, spewing mud behind them. On either side of the truck was Quickdraw's jacked-up navy blue Chevy, and Two Shots white truck. They were skidding this way and that through the trees. Their tires made big divots in the mud.

Beside her, Dead was turning the wheel expertly, navigating the trees with his back-end fishtailing back and forth.

This was okay. Everything was all right.

Through the trees, there was a clearing, and Dead pointed the nose of the truck toward an opening through two massive pines. Quickdraw was already in the clearing, right on the edge, stopped and revving his engine.

"Little shit thinks he has a chance in a Chevy," Dead said through a laugh.

His eyes were bright green and dancing every time he glanced at her. "I've got you," he said suddenly as he pulled up next to Quickdraw.

She nodded jerkily and grabbed onto the oh-shit handle above the door. "Just live."

His grin turned straight wicked. "Atta girl."

On Dead's other side, Two Shots pulled up, and the passenger window rolled down. Cheyenne stood up out of the window, threw her arms out, and yelled at the sky. Pretty Cheyenne was even prettier with that free spirit leaking out. Maybe that's where extra beauty came from. Letting go of control gave a person a different aura.

Cheyenne finished her howl and pointed at Dead. "You're going down."

Dead revved his engine loudly as Cheyenne scrambled back into the passenger seat and began rolling up her window.

There was a loaded moment when Dead was looking on either side of him at the trucks all lined up. Quickdraw hit the gas first, and Dead whooped as he gunned it. One hand on the wheel, one hand slipping to her tensed thigh, he drove them straight across that clearing. The problem was, there were puddles. They would get bogged down, and Dead would have to correct, but the same was happening to Two Shots and Quickdraw, and by the time they were midway through the field, Raven was cracking up and yelling encouragement. "This way, this way, this way!" she whooped as Two Shots had to veer to the right to avoid a tuft of brush. His movement gave them just enough room to skirt a deep muddy bog.

"Oh, yeah, I see it," Dead murmured, heading for the gap.

Raven couldn't stop laughing as adrenaline surged through her. Her skin tingled, and her breath caught in her chest as they almost, almost, hit the brush. Oh, Dead could drive. His wheels had come less than an inch from the branches of the foliage, and then he gunned it.

Two Shots was struggling to get out of a mud pit, and Quickdraw had made it out front. He cut sharply and settled in front of Dead.

"I don't think so, Quickdick," he muttered, taking his hand from Raven's thigh to turn the wheel sharp. He aimed for a slope on the left and caught better traction. He was still fishtailing, but he was going fast enough now that it made her stomach do a flip like she was on a roller coaster.

She was yelling for him, cheering for him as they caught up to Quickdraw, who was now on their right.

He flipped them off out the window, and Dead did the same to him just as he found another gear and blasted past him on higher, drier ground. They made it to the edge of the clearing first, but Dead wasn't done. When he cut hard to the right, his back end spun out. They spun in circle after circle, spraying a rooster tail of mud as Raven held onto the oh-shit bar for dear life, her breath trapped in her throat. Dead was yelling a victory battle cry as they spun and spun and spun. When he slowed and came out of the donut, Quickdraw was doing a wide loop around them and Two Shots was doing donuts in the middle of the field. It was like a dance.

"God, I love this," she huffed out, shaking with excitement and adrenaline.

"Your eyes," Dead said as they rocked to a stop.

She searched his bright green ones. "What about them?"

He reached over and stroked his thumb gently across her cheek. "They're beautiful."

Confused, she popped down the sun visor and looked in the little mirror there. Her eyes were black as pitch. There wasn't any white at all.

"Oh no," she whispered, looking away. "I didn't— I don't—"

"You aren't going to change," Dead said with such confidence. "You're going to keep having fun. You don't even smell like fur. Your animal is having fun."

Raven didn't feel as sure as he sounded, though. She'd never gotten what she called "the demon eyes" and not changed before.

He leaned over suddenly and kissed her. Hand on the back of her neck, squeezing comfortingly, he moved his lips against hers, and that racing heartbeat of hers slowed.

He drew back and rested his forehead on hers.

"It's just me and you. Having fun. And if you got to the point where you had to change? Okay. That's natural, and I won't let anyone hurt you."

Raven forced the words past her tightening vocal cords. "It's not me I would worry about."

His lips curved up in a handsome smile. "Then I wouldn't let you hurt anyone. You trust me?"

She nodded. "I shouldn't trust a stranger, but I do."

Dead snorted. "Woman, you can't use the stranger excuse anymore. I've met your parents. Now, hold onto your panties. We have company."

"Company?" Her confusion lasted until she followed his gaze to the other side of the clearing they'd just raced across.

Four more trucks appeared out of the tree line. Five. Six. It must've been the other bulls and cowboys staying in the RV park.

"Ready to have some fun?" Dead asked.

Quickdraw had stopped right beside them. His truck was caked with mud, and his wipers were slowly scraping the thick stuff off his front windshield. He was facing the new players and revved his engine.

"I see 'em!" Quickdraw called.

In front of them, Two Shots was bogged down in mud and had gotten out to push while Cheyenne was behind the wheel and had the driver's side door open, yelling directions to him and giving the truck some gas.

"Let's go help them!" Raven said.

"Yes ma'am!" Dead hit the gas and made it to them in seconds. Quickdraw, too.

The boys skidded to a stop, and Raven, Dead, and Quickdraw bolted out of the trucks. The mud was shin-deep and hard to move in, but this was a rare benefit to being a cow shifter. Raven was strong.

"Need a big push!" Cheyenne yelled.

The other trucks were slipping and sliding toward them, and time wasn't on their side!

Panting, Cheyenne slogged through the muck in her motorcycle boots, the boys on either side, and put her hands on the bumper.

"Hit the gas when we say!" Two shots called.

"One!" Dead yelled. "Two! Three!"

Raven put all her weight into that push, fear fueling her. Those trucks were getting closer. Too close!

The boys beside her pushed, too, and the truck moved. Forward...forward.

"Keep pushing!" Two Shots ordered.

Raven barely kept her balance as she pulled her boots through that deep mud, and it was hard to keep up. The bull shifters beside her drove with their powerful legs, and the tires caught traction.

"Keep going, don't stop!" Two Shots told Cheyenne.

And she did. She forced that truck right out of the bog, at the expense of slinging mud all over Raven and the boys.

Dead shielded her with his body, hugged her close until the mud stopped spraying, but she was already a mess.

And when she opened her eyes and looked up at him, his grin was reaching all the way to his bright eyes. "You look so hot when you're dirty."

Whatever she'd expected him to say, it wasn't that, and she had no idea how to respond with those loud trucks getting closer, so she sloshed up on her tiptoes and kissed him quick. She gasped when he picked her up and tossed her over his shoulder. She laughed breathlessly as he ran clumsily out of the mud hole to his truck, his boots making sucking, squishy noises with every step. Quickdraw was doing the same thing, and that man still didn't have a shirt on. His outfit was now *couture de mud*.

She waved at Cheyenne, but her new friend had her phone up taking pictures. Oh, yeah, lovely. Raven definitely, probably, looked like a super model right about now.

She bounced hard as Dead started jogging toward the truck on dryer land. All six trucks had reached them and were circling, spraying mud. Dead and Raven scrambled into the truck, and Dead yelled, "Hell, yeah, here we go!" as he hit the gas and turned them away from the muddy bog Two Shots had been stuck in.

The next hour went by in a snap. It was full of yelling and cheering and cussing when they got too close to other trucks. It was full of muddy fishtails and Dead slipping his hand to her thigh on every straightaway. It was full of good old boys hanging out of passenger windows and pairs of trucks pulling off to rest and chat while they watched the chaos in the muddy field.

Dead didn't seem to care that she was getting

mud on his seats. He just seemed happy. At ease, and after his dream last night, seeing him like this in his element loosened something inside her heart.

Could a woman fall in love with a man in a day? Could a shifter?

It was hard to look away from him, from the smile on his face, and his happiness filled her insides with something big. That man was utterly consuming.

Fun boy.

Tough boy.

Hilarious boy.

Didn't-get-knocked-down-for-long boy.

Caring boy.

Her boy...

Dead didn't know it yet, and she would be slow about revealing her feelings, but she thought something mighty big about him.

"You falling in love?" he asked suddenly as he was easing into a muddy turn.

Rattled that he'd read her mind, she blurted out, "What?"

"The way you keep lookin' at me. You falling in love?"

Her cheeks, her cheeks, her damn flaming cheeks.

She pressed her fingertips there and looked out the window to hide from him. "Focus on driving, wild man. You promised to keep me safe."

He didn't say anything, but when she dared a glance back at him, he had this knowing little smile on his face.

"Oh, hush," she muttered.

"I didn't say anything," he told her innocently.

Dead pulled off the main muddy drag and headed for the RV park. He pulled up to Two Shots' truck that was headed in the opposite direction. Two Shots rolled down his window. "Where are y'all going?"

"I'm gonna get this one in the shower and take her to breakfast before we have to hit the road."

"Did you have fun?" Cheyenne called to Raven from the passenger seat.

"Honestly? I don't think I've ever had so much fun in my life!"

Dead was beaming as he waved and drove off. "You're so freakin' fun," he told her when they reached the RV park. "I know you were nervous at first, but you tried it, and now look at you."

She looked down at herself, covered in mud and filth. She couldn't even read the Battle of the Bulls logo on her cut-up T-shirt anymore. "I've seen muddin' on movies, but never thought about it being like that. We were going so fast."

"Watching stuff on TV is different than living it."

"Well, I know that's true. My life is like a movie right now."

He pulled up to his camper and backed it right up to the hitch like a pro. "What do you mean?"

"I mean I'm supposed to be arranging flowers right now, like I do every other day. It's Monday, so I would cook Monday spaghetti, check on my plants, watch the same competitive cooking show I watch every week, and then would be in bed by nine. Rinse and repeat every Monday. Instead, I'm still on a high from the rodeo last night, figuring my animal out a little better, I'm covered in mud, and I've now been on the inside of a real camper."

"And slept in it. While being the little spoon to my big spoon. And you forgot the most important part of a romantic comedy."

"Mmm hmm, and what's that?"

"You met me—a gallant, strapping, bearded, hilarious hero who can cook and who has the perfect balance of good boy and bad boy with a massive dick—"

"Dead!" she choked out. Escape was her only option to get out of the embarrassment, so she pushed open the door and became very busy with stomping mud off her boots.

"The shower is all hooked up and will warm up after a few minutes," he called from behind the truck where he was messing with the hitch. "Just drop your clothes in a pile out here, and I'll rinse them off."

"Oh. Okay. I feel kind of bad for not helping clean."

He stood up straight with a frown drawing his blond brows down. "You want to help?"

"Why wouldn't I? It's not fair that you do all the work."

His expression relaxed, his eyes softened, and the confusion faded away. "I like you."

Her stomach clenched and released, and an accidental smile ghosted her lips. "Really?"

"Yep. I really do. You're shy but funny, quiet but with a quick wit. You have confidence in surprising moments, and it's so damn attractive. You're beautiful, obviously, but I like more than that. Your parents are nice, and I can tell you're close. I like that you're a family girl. You're a hard worker, and you don't expect things of other people. You offer to help. And you say 'thank you' if anyone does anything for you and, nowadays, those traits are rare. And surprising in a good way. I haven't found anything I don't like about you yet, and I've been lookin'. You're just a good woman."

Raven pursed her lips and kicked at a mud clump with the toe of her boot. Had she ever felt so good about herself in any given moment? She couldn't recall.

"Thank you for those compliments." And then softly, she admitted, "I like you, too."

TEN

The shower wasn't warming up.

Cold water splashed across her open palm as Raven checked it for the tenth time. Cold showers weren't her favorite, but her skin was speckled with mud and grit and her hair was drying in a dirty mat on her head, so a cold shower it would be.

Dead knocked. "We can do a laundromat date tonight when we stop if you want."

She smiled and snuggled the towel a little tighter around her, then pulled the door open.

He was leaning against the door frame, both arms locked on either side. His vibrant blue eyes dragged down her fuzzy white towel to her mud-splattered legs and back up.

"I've never had a laundromat date before."

"A virgin." He straightened up. "I accept the pressure of popping your cherry. I'll do the LD justice."

She snorted and rolled her eyes, tested the water again.

He frowned at the shower. "Is it not heating up?"

"I think it's broken."

"Let me check the water heater. Hang on." Dead disappeared for a minute and then reappeared in the doorway again. "Two minutes, and it should be heating up now."

"Oh, my goodness, yay. Nothing sounds better than a warm shower to get this gunk out of my hair." She raised a crusted mud dread up into the air. "I like to seduce you by showing you my worst and then dressing up for you later. I like to set the bar very low, and then when you have zero expectations, I dazzle you and brush my hair. I'm breaking you in."

"Mmmm," he rumbled, filling up the entire bathroom. He slipped his hands to her waist and gripped the towel. "How about we skip the dressing up later. Maybe I like you just like this."

His eyes were full of such honesty, the self-deprecating jokes fell from her lips. "Really?"

His smile was crooked under that beard of his. Crooked and handsome and genuine. She loved his smile. He gifted them to her so easily.

He cupped her neck and ran his thumb gently under her eye. "I like that you can get dirty without complaining. That you can loosen up and have fun. It's sexy."

Raven slid her hand down his forearm to his wrist and squeezed. She didn't want him to pull away.

He eased her back until she was pressed against the edge of the sink, right by the shower. Slowly, he pulled her towel away from her and tossed it behind him. With the back of his forefinger, he drew a line along her collarbone and then down, down to trace her breast. Raven let off a trembling sigh and a small shiver at how good it felt to be touched.

His hand was strong as he cupped her tit, massaged, then melted her completely when he massaged the other. His fingertips trailed fire where he explored. Streaks of warmth down her ribs to the curve of her waist to her hips. Dead looked at her skin like he was memorizing it. Memorizing every curve, slope, indentation. Every freckle. Every tattoo.

The look in his eyes filled her stomach with a happy fluttering sensation. She was beautiful to him. She could tell in the hungry look on his face and the smile that curved up just slightly when he brushed her hair off her shoulder and traced her jaw line. Time and time again, he moved back to her breasts, kneading them until she was putty in his capable hands.

There wasn't an ounce of rush on his time. Raven's shyness faded as the minutes wore on, and she settled into a comfort she'd never known before.

"May I?" she whispered, tugging at the hem of his T-shirt.

He nodded. No words here. Not right now. He lifted his arms, and she peeled his shirt over his head. She blew out a steadying breath as she studied him, too. The hair on his defined chest was so light. When she ran her fingertips across it, Dead rolled his eyes closed and shivered. He was so much bigger than her, taking up most of the small bathroom, but he seemed content, just like this, while petting each other.

She wanted more, but not too fast. Not too fast. This wasn't some quick treat and then done. She knew down to her bones this was different than anything she'd ever experienced with a man. It was special. It was bonding an animal to an animal. It was bonding a heart to a heart.

He cupped her cheeks and watched her face as she traced the deep lines of his muscles. The one between his pecs, the ones between his abs, the ones at that sexy hip muscle that delved into his jeans. She hugged him and traced the thick muscle on either side of his spine, and he shivered again. This time, he elicited a deep rumbling sound that called to her animal, too. Ooooh, beautiful, sexy boy. She was in trouble with him.

She reached between his thighs and groaned when her hand landed on his thick, stone-hard shaft.

He reached into the shower and felt the water, then eased her into the small space. It wasn't a big shower, but he stripped out of his jeans and stepped right in after her, then pulled a washrag off a shelf. He began rubbing the abrasive cloth gently across her wet skin. She leaned back, wetting her hair as he cleaned her. Nothing had ever felt so good in all her life. His hand holding her waist still, his other cleaning her skin, his eyes tracing the washcloth with a hungry look. The water was steaming but not too hot, and when he was finished, she took the cloth from him and began to wash his skin, too.

She'd never been a part of something more intimate. He turned for her, and she ran the cloth down his muscular back. On the floor below their feet, muddy water ran into the drain. When the water ran clear, he turned toward her and poured shampoo into his hand, and then massaged her scalp until she was moaning, her head tilted back and her eyes closed. His fingers felt so good. And while she rinsed her hair out under the hot water, he went to kissing her. Kissing her lips, her throat, and then he bent low enough to pull her nipple into his mouth. She gasped as he sucked hard, then leaned into it and gripped the back of his hair.

"Dead," she whispered, and that seemed to be enough for him.

He folded her into his arms and squeezed out of the bathroom, made his way up the three stairs to the bed and laid her on it. They were both slick with water, and he settled in between her legs as his lips brushed hers. She spread her knees wider for him, and she could feel the head of his cock right there at her wet entrance.

Dead pressed against her. She ran her nails

through his hair and kissed him harder. She wrapped her legs around his strong waist and with a grunt, he slid into her. There was no stopping the storm they'd started now. It felt too good. Felt too right. He thrust into her with deep strokes, and her body sang with pleasure, building and building as he rolled his hips into hers.

She was making noises, but Raven couldn't help herself; she was mindless. He'd made her lose all coherent thought. All that existed was this pressure they were building. God, he felt so good, gliding into her, then out, in and out, faster, harder. Her tits were smashed against his chest, his tongue was thrusting deep inside her mouth, and she was holding onto him for dear life because she was about to break apart.

Felt so good, soooo good, so right, so perfect. She tossed her head back and cried out, and his teeth grazed her neck as he slammed into her. And then he pulled back fast, shoved her knees to her chest and held them there, his darkening eyes locked on hers. He bucked into her harder.

Never would she forget the sight of his strong, muscular body pounding against hers like this. Never would she forget his abs and chest and arms flexing with every pump, or the way he looked at her like he owned her soul.

Her orgasm was throbbing through her, so intense, and he was slamming into her so fast now. She yelled his name with how good he felt dragging her release out. He pushed in, grunted, and spilled wet heat into her.

She never wanted it to end.

Apparently, Dead didn't either because he stayed there, covering her, settled between her legs, his comforting weight on top of her. And then he kissed her for a long time. Kissed and touched her, not in any rush to disconnect from her.

They didn't need words here for what they'd done or the bond they'd created. They spoke with their fingertips.

Dead didn't know it yet, but with every caring touch, he was making her his.

ELEVEN

Five hours into the road trip, Two Shots, leading their caravan, pulled off the highway.

Raven pointed to the exit sign as they passed. "Exit sixty-nine."

"We should do that tonight. Exit sixty-nine, I feel like it's a sign," Dead said. "See how I rhymed that?"

"Yeah, your whole career revolves around poetry." She pointed to the shirt she wore, two sizes too big and tied at her waist. On it was a picture of the stands at some rodeo, and smack-dab in the middle was a woman holding a sign that read *Dead, Dead, he's good in bed*.

"Oh, it's fun to read what the fans come up with. Dead, Dead, you have a big head. Dead, Dead, he's an inbred. That one came from someone who wasn't a fan of mine," he explained with a chuckle. Dead leaned an elbow against the window frame and draped one hand over the steering wheel. "Dead, Dead, he don't eat bread. Dead, Dead, was it something I said? Dead, Dead, he's seein' red. Dead, Dead, horns full of lead. Dead, Dead, take us both home instead."

"Let me guess. From two female fans?"

He took a right behind where Two Shots had turned in front of them. "Yep."

Raven tried to make her voice nonchalant as she asked, "And did you take them home?"

"Hell no. One woman is enough. Y'all are crazy. I'm not doing double the work."

She snickered and smacked his arm lightly. "We're not that bad."

"No, *you* aren't that bad. Every other female I've met? Work."

"Maybe you just don't have patience for us."

"No." His tone went serious and he cast a bright-eyed glance at her. "No, that ain't it. There's a saying in the industry. If you get paired up, it takes away from your drive. You start worrying about being home and the mate you have waiting up for you. You start checkin' your phone more, focusing on building a relationship, and you lose the drive to buck."

"I didn't think of that." She drew her feet under her, crossing her legs. "I can see how that would be true, though. Relationships take a lot of work, a lot of energy, and right now all your energy is going into your career. It would shake things up for sure."

Dead shrugged up a shoulder and slowed his truck behind Two Shots, whose brake lights had come on the camper he was pulling. "I used to believe that so I steered clear of anything serious on purpose. Anyone got too close, I gave them the boot. I kept all my walls up and kept blinders on so I could just get through each week bucking and improve. I didn't want anyone to take my focus off what I wanted to do."

"Do you still believe a woman will kill your career?"

"Nope."

"Why not?" Curiosity might have killed the cat, but she was a cow, and there weren't any sayings about that.

Dead gestured up ahead of them to where Two

Shots was taking a right onto a dirt road. "Being around Two Shots and Cheyenne changed my mind. She doesn't let him lose focus, and now he has something bigger to buck for. Something outside of himself. He wants to buy her a ring. A pretty ring like she deserves. A big flashy one. And not just a ring. He wants to give her a life. A good life. He talked to me and Quickdraw about it, and now he's been holding onto top two bull in the world and getting paid. And Cheyenne pushes him in good ways. She doesn't take his crap, doesn't get soft when he's sore or tweaks something. She tells him to buck up. So now, I think that a female wouldn't be so bad if it were the right fit."

"The right fit," she repeated softly.

"Yeah. If she inspired a bull and pushed him in the right direction. Propped him up when he had his quiet, weak moments. Any insecurities, tell him to fuck off and get back to work. Stuff like that."

"I don't think I could tell you to fuck off ever."

"You saying you aren't cut out for it?"

Honestly, after he'd explained all that...she wasn't so sure. She had a very different personality than Cheyenne. "I don't know."

"I met a stranger who bought me a beer and stopped what she was doing to help me at a table. You did all the little work that takes away from my quality time with fans, and you never asked for payment, credit, or attention for it. You were fine just being in the background helping me and Cheyenne. And then you made yourself at home in my kitchen and helped me cook without me asking. You accepted my friends and fit right in with them, but you know what you haven't done yet?"

"What?"

Readjusting, he pulled her hand from her lap and kissed her knuckle. "Asked me *why* I buck or when will I quit this career."

"Oh." She smiled shyly. "It never crossed my mind that you would stop. It's part of you. What right would I have to take away something you obviously love?"

His eyebrows arched up high. "So what were you saying about not making a good teammate?"

"Teammate?"

"Well, if I call you 'girlfriend,' you'll get that shut-down look in your eye because the logical part of you is pretty big, and you think it's too soon for me to like you this much without some other shoe about to drop. So, we'll go at your pace. Slow as a fuckin' snail for me, but I get it."

"Teammate. Or partner. I like that. It means neither one of us is putting in more effort than the other."

"Exactly. Neither one of us is less important than the other. I've never had that before, and I want to see where this goes. First up?" He jerked his chin toward a clearing with a big corral and bucking chutes right in the middle of it. "You get to relax and just watch a workout. And knowing me, I'll probably go harder because a pretty girl is watching me."

"Chhh, I'll be out there drinking a White Claw with Cheyenne. She bought us a whole case when we stopped at the last gas station."

"Girl, that is so sexy," he said with a chuckle as he pulled to a stop alongside the practice arena.

"You're so easy to please. Mud on my tits and a White Claw in my hand, and you're ready to go."

"You're damn right. That's my fantasy right there. Anytime you want this dick, you just dress in mud and White Claws."

She giggled at the mental picture of her sitting on

a lawn chair caked in mud, drinkin' and waggling her eyebrows seductively at Dead. The man possessed the perfect level of weird.

"I got you something at the gas station, too," he said mysteriously as he opened his door.

"A present?" she asked, slipping out of the passenger side of his truck.

"Yep!"

He pulled a long cylinder-shaped bag out of the bed of his truck and climbed the ladder that led to the roof of his camper. She couldn't see what he was doing from this angle so close to the camper, but when she started to back up to get a better view, Dead told her, "Don't look yet."

Well, okay. What was that man up to?

She shoved her red gas station sunglasses farther up her nose and watched Cheyenne pour some kind of liquor out of a flask and give the shot glass to Two Shots. A pre-buck ritual perhaps?

Cheyenne gave him two shots, took one for herself, and then lifted the flask and glass to Raven. "Want one?"

"No thanks. It's a little early for the hard stuff."

"That's what she said," Dead called from the roof

of the camper. "Okay, come on up! Cheyenne, toss me one of them girly drinks you been icing down."

Raven scaled the ladder, and when she got to the top, she grinned so big. He'd set up a camp chair with a big umbrella and faced it to the arena.

Dead stood there with his legs splayed and his hands on his hips, looking like a proud peacock and, good gracious, she'd never seen a man look hotter.

Today he was wearing a V-neck black T-shirt, wranglers that hugged his muscular legs just right, and his worn boots. His muscles were popping out everywhere and, damn, that tattoo down his arm sure looked yummy.

"You like it?"

"Y-yes," she stuttered. "The chair and..." She waved her hand around at him.

"I'm the total package, baby." A White Claw came sailing over the side of the camper that he caught without his eyes ever leaving Raven's. And then he popped the top and offered it to her with the most charming smirk she'd ever witnessed on a man's face.

Raven scaled the rest of the ladder and hoisted herself onto the top of the camper. After she took the drink from Dead, he held out his hand again, and an energy drink landed in it. He still hadn't broken the stare-off with Raven.

"Okay, that was awesome," Cheyenne called from below. "Good catches!"

"Mediocre throws," Dead kind-of complimented her back.

"Uuuh, thanks?" Cheyenne said. "I think?"

He popped the top of his energy drink and did a toast. "To your perfect tits."

"Oh, my gosh," Raven murmured, mortified.

"Not a good toast? Fine. To your perfect tits and also your voluptuous vagin—"

"Okay!" Raven tinked her drink against his and took a healthy swig.

Dead chugged the whole drink, threw down the frothing can off the side, kissed Raven fast, and then jumped off the camper.

She screamed and bolted to the edge, but he was fine. The man was already walking toward the arena, peeling off his shirt.

"Where are you going?" she asked. "Two Shots is about to buck!" The white bull was already loaded in a chute, and though she didn't know much about her kind, she knew bulls were volatile around each other.

"I'm going to fight Quickdraw."

"Wait, what?" she yelled after him.

Cheyenne came over the top of the camper, a bag chair on her shoulder and a small cooler in her other hand. "He said he's going to fight Quickdraw. Hey!" she called after him. "Be careful of your faces. We have a photoshoot this week."

"No, no, no, no!" Raven exclaimed. "Why are they fighting? They're friends!"

Cheyenne pulled the chair out of her bag. It was navy blue with little colorful llamas all over it. "Oh, they always fight. Quickdraw needs it before a buck. He needs blood, Dead needs energy drinks, and Two Shots needs two shots."

"What kinda man needs blood before a buck?" she asked, horrified.

As Dead approached Quickdraw leaning against the arena gate, Quickdraw straightened up with his fists clenched, an evil smile on his face.

"The kind that's half-devil." Cheyenne frowned at them as Dead threw a punch. "Want some cheese crackers?"

"Um, no thank you." Raven clapped a hand over her mouth as Dead blasted a fist across Quickdraw's face, and she mumbled, "I don't have much of an appetite."

Crunching loudly on the snacks, Cheyenne relaxed back into her llama chair and assured her, "That'll change. You'll be used to all this in no time."

But as Raven stared out over the scene before her—Two Shots' massive bull bucking in the arena like there was no tomorrow, and Quickdraw and the man she loved beating the ever-living stuffing out of each other just below—she seriously doubted what Cheyenne said.

There was no getting used to this.

TWELVE

"I could get used to this," Raven said, clinking her can against Cheyenne's.

They'd both changed into clearance swimsuits they'd bought at a Walmart a couple towns back. Nothing was left in the cheese cracker package but crumbs.

"It's not a bad life," Cheyenne concurred.

Dead had just finished his last practice buck, the last of the three to take a turn in the arena. Quickdraw was sitting on a rickety wooden bench with a pulse machine hooked up to his right bicep, and the thing made his muscles jump every second in a rhythm. Two Shots was putting his clothes back on and Dead, well, Dead was as naked as a sled—oof, she was bad at rhyming.

He was hiding his southern parts with two cupped hands. He called up to her, "You wanna buck?"

Okay, she must've misheard him. "Haha, I thought you asked if I want to buck."

"I did."

"But she's a cow," Quickdraw enlightened him.

"No shit, Sherlock, I'm gonna call you Slowdraw now."

Quickdraw jerked forward like he was going to attack Dead as he passed, but Dead didn't flinch. Instead, he came to a stop under the camper and leaned his head back, gripping his hips.

"Dead, put some clothes on!" Cheyenne demanded.

"Nudity is natural," Dead told her.

"I second that," Quickdraw said, ripping the electrodes off his arm.

"I don't second it," Two Shots griped. "My lady doesn't need to see your sausage and beans."

"Did you really trim your balls but ignore the entire section in your contract about keeping your hair and beard trimmed?" Cheyenne asked, leaning over the edge of the camper.

"I trimmed my hair. You didn't specify which hair. Contract abided by."

"She meant your head hair, you dick!" Two Shots blurted out.

Raven lowered to her belly so she could safely look over the side. She kicked her legs in the air and smiled. "I like that you manscape."

Puffing up like a proud turkey, Dead looked at the other boys and then flipped them off, one by one.

Raven was already in a fit of giggles by the time she saw their pissed-off faces.

"I was being serious." Dead pulled his pair of jeans off the bed of his truck and came back to stand right under Raven. "Do you want to buck?"

"But...why would I?"

"To get a change in. To ease some of the tension from your animal. To give her a good workout. To maybe settle some of her intensity. There's lots of reasons to buck. It's good for you."

"Really, he just wants to see your cow," Quickdraw told her as he clenched his fist a few times, testing his arm.

"Admission, I kind of want to see it, too,"

Cheyenne said.

"Oh, no, no, no. No one wants to see that. She's...my animal... Well, she's not in control like you boys' animals."

Dead gestured to the arena behind him. "This ranch is owned by a shifter. These panels are reinforced for bull shifters, and the chutes are bigger to fit us. It's about as safe an environment as you can give her."

He made good points, but her heart was already pounding against her sternum just thinking about doing something as embarrassing as changing in front of her new friends. She wanted them to keep liking her.

"Your cheeks are turning red," Dead pointed out.

"Well, don't look then," she squeaked out, scuttling away from the edge. She sat on the camper roof and drew her knees in, staring at the arena. If she did this, they wouldn't ever look at her the same. "I don't change in front of people."

"Why not?" Dead asked, his head popping over the edge of the camper at the ladder.

"You're pushing me," she murmured low.

"I'm not. You can say no, and it'll be perfectly fine.

But if we get ten miles down the road, and you're still thinking about it—and I'm onto you, you're an overthinker—I don't want you to regret not taking the chance. Nobody here even has the capacity to judge you. Two Shots is as dumb as a barn, Quickdraw has probably killed a dozen people, and Cheyenne is boning the man who killed her late husband. What can they say about your cow? I'm the perfect specimen of a man, but I'm not judgmental, sooo…"

"Jump off a cliff," Quickdraw muttered to him in a bored voice.

"Look, my animal isn't like yours," she whispered.

"Good. I'm bored of seeing the same old shit. Go surprise us, Raven. I'll make it okay. I'll keep her in the arena."

"We all will," Two Shots called from down by the gate. "Come on, girl, let us see what you got."

She looked up at Cheyenne, who was sitting just a few feet away from her. Could she tell how scared Raven was? Could she tell?

Cheyenne nodded supportively, but her tone was stern. "Go show them boys what you're made of."

She swallowed hard. Would she regret it ten

miles down the road? If she chickened out with all of them watching, would she lay awake thinking about it tonight? Dead was probably right. She probably would.

Just get it over with.

Inside of her, the animal stirred, and her skin began to tingle.

Slow and steady, she made her way to the ladder and climbed down. Eyes averted, she made her way to the gate where Two Shots was holding it open.

"You got this. Bucking is easy. Just don't think about anything. Just get pissed and let it out."

Dead appeared beside her, a rope in his hand as they walked across the arena toward a holding pen on the other side where she could change. "Think of someone you hate."

"I don't hate anyone," she murmured.

"Your cow? Does she hate?"

"Oh. The animal is different."

"She hates everyone, doesn't she?"

Jerkily, Raven nodded. "Hates *everything*. That fence?" she asked, pointing to the tall panels. "She'll hate it. That fly? She'll hate it. This dirt?" She kicked some with the toe of her boot. "She'll hate it. You?"

She couldn't finish that part. The words got stuck in her throat because they didn't feel right.

He finished it for her. "She'll hate me. That's okay. It won't be like that forever. She just has to get to know me and figure out I won't ever hurt her. When you're changed, think of someone or something you hate and imagine that someone or something clinging to your back. Using you. Heckling you. Gonna benefit off holding on. This is *your* arena," he growled. "Don't let anything stay on your back."

"I'm not a bull though, Dead," she whispered.

"What the hell does that have to do with anything?"

"Cows don't buck."

"Yeah, well, maybe that's because nobody ever asked a cow to do it." He gave her a swift smack on the ass. "Own your wild."

Own her wild? She wasn't wild. She had pet plants and a steady bedtime.

That's not how she changed into her animal. Changing was a careful process with planning and safety measures involved. Owning her wild was out of the question. If he knew her animal, he wouldn't put that dare on the table. To keep everyone safe, she had to change in a big barn on her parent's property that had been reinforced at every wall.

This was a bad idea. It was a stupid, irresponsible, no-good, awful, bad idea. But if ever she was going to try a bad idea, then she supposed this was the place to do it. Surely, three mature bulls could get her animal in line.

Maybe.

****

Dead closed her into the holding pen and gave her his back. "Everything will be great, Raven. You'll see. No one's even looking over here, so you can change in peac—"

A ground-shaking bawl sounded from behind him and startled him so bad he hunched his shoulders and pressed his hands to his ears as he spun. It sounded like a damn foghorn and rattled his chest with the power of it.

And what stood behind that gate was the likes of which he'd never seen before.

Raven wasn't Raven any longer. The fury...the rage, the hatred that wafted from that animal, clogged his throat and made it hard to breath. She stared at him through the metal slats. He couldn't see much of her body with the gate between them. All he knew was she was black as pitch, and her eyes matched. Her horns stretched straight out to the side and curved up, with twists at the sharp ends like handlebars. They were white with black tips.

Dead had never been scared of anything in his adult life, but Raven's animal was conjured straight from hell. She bellowed low, and then in a flash, she slammed her head against the gate of the holding pen with such force, the metal bent toward him.

"Dead!" Two Shots yelled. "Get her into the chute!"

"Holy fucking shit, what is that?" Quickdraw panted as he ran along the fence to undo the gate that separated the holding pen from the alleyway to the chutes.

She slammed her head against the gate again, and the metal groaned and bent more. The latch was holding on by so little, but Dead was frozen in her glare. She paced to the back of the holding area and turned to charge the gate. It wouldn't hold.

"Dead, move!" Cheyenne screamed from somewhere behind him.

"Shhhhit," he cursed as he forced himself to get

out of the way of the gate.

She stopped mid charge and spun, and as Dead scrambled up onto the fence to tempt her into the chutes, he saw why she'd stopped. Two Shots had jumped into the pen with her.

He almost didn't make it out. Raven charged faster than a snake strike. Her massive horns didn't seem to weigh her down at all, and she wasn't built like other cows he'd seen. She had more muscle, more mass, and aggression seeped out of every pore. Hagan. That's what had done this to her. She had that dark Hagan blood pumping through her veins.

Two Shots had to leap over the fence, no time to climb it. She hit it hard, and the metal made a gong sound that rattled Dead's head and nearly shook him off the fence.

"Come on, Raven. Come on!" Dead shouted.

Quickdraw was whistling. He'd climbed into the alleyway, baiting her. She went for it, charged straight for him, but she had to turn her head so her long horns could fit, and it gave Quickdraw time to run. She followed him right into a chute.

"Get out of there!" Cheyenne screamed as Quickdraw scrambled up the chute fencing.

Raven barely missed his leg. When Dead slammed closed the back of the chute, she kicked it so hard, he went flying off the metal.

Quickdraw had a rope agitating her neck, as if she needed it. Raven was pinned in the small space. She let off another foghorn bellow. Dead and Two Shots barely got the flank rope on her without being mauled.

"Does she even need this?" Two Shots yelled.

"Fuck if I know. She's the size of a dinosaur! Let's just get her out of here. She don't like being pinned."

Quickdraw rushed to the arena, readied the rope on the gate to pull it open. "Tell me when!" he shouted, his face red, sweat trickling down his temple.

"Tighten it quick before she breaks this whole chute, man," Two Shots murmured low.

Fumbling, Dead tightened it, careful to keep it higher up her belly.

"Pull it!" Dead yelled.

And when he did, time became different. It became slow. Two Shots was yelling, Cheyenne was running along the fence shouting orders, Quickdraw was pulling on that rope, and his sweet Raven owned her wild.

That monster cow shifter followed that opening gate with no hesitation. She leapt out of there and went to bucking so hard the arena dust made a cloud. He could feel the vibration of every powerful buck she did.

No one spoke. They just froze and watched as Raven caught air and kicked back. She was flying. Her horns had to be heavy, but they didn't seem to have any effect on her bucking. She went for fifteen seconds, easy, and when she slowed, she trotted out to the middle of the arena, doing little bunny bucks of her back end. She didn't like the rope, and he got it. That flank rope was designed to agitate.

"We gotta get it off her boys!" Dead called.

So he and Two Shots and Quickdraw hopped into the arena with the beast.

She stood still, looking from him to the others and back to him. The tattoos showed. God, the tattoos. They were a few shades darker than her short black fur, and when she turned, sweat glistening off her hide. He could just make out the lines. They weren't the same shape as her human form. No, in this form, they looked like black lace across her flank.

The boys worked as a team. She charged Quickdraw first because he was the closest, so Two Shots ran in front of her face while Quickdraw ran. Dead swerved in and pulled the release on the flank strap, which fell to the earth.

Raven spun and charged Dead.

There wasn't enough time to get away. Not enough time.

Two Shots and Quickdraw were yelling something, Cheyenne too, but he couldn't make it out through the roar in his ears. He turned to run, but he wouldn't be fast enough.

Gasping, he turned and tensed his legs. He had no other choice but to jump over her, hoping her tossing head wouldn't hook him with one of her horns.

"It's okay." He didn't know why he told her that right now, but it felt important. This wasn't Raven. This animal had nothing to do with the sweet girl he'd fallen for.

It's okay. Those were the words she'd first uttered to him in the rodeo arena. The words that made him stop to think about what he was doing.

The monstrous, pitch-black animal locked her legs against her forward motion, her glossy black hooves digging into the arena dirt as she halted.

She stopped inches from his boots, her head at his chest. Three breaths was all she blew before she morphed into her human skin with a barrage of pops. A black cloud of smoke enveloped her but slowly cleared to reveal his Raven—pale-skinned, tattooed, wild-haired, round-eyed Raven, panting as she crossed her arms over her chest and stared up at him.

"I'm sorry," she whispered.

And there was a loaded moment when no one said anything. One loaded piece of time when everyone stared at her with what-the-hell-just-happened looks on their faces.

And then Dead let off a whoop, and the others went off at the same time.

"That was awesome!" Dead told her as the others were cheering and freaking out around them. He fell to his knees in the dirt in front of her and yanked off his shirt. He pulled it down over her head and dragged her against his chest. Even Cheyenne was screaming something about "the coolest thing she'd ever seen!"

"You never have to be sorry, Raven. You shouldn't be sorry for her."

"For her," she repeated shakily as she sat there, melted against Dead's rocking body.

"Oh, yeah, your cow is totally separate from you. She's not Raven. She's Other."

"Other, other," she chanted, her body shaking with adrenaline.

Dead rubbed warmth into her arms. "What's her name?"

Raven shrugged, her eyes round with shock. "I don't know."

"Her name is Lace then," Dead murmured, still on a high from the look of her tattooed hide.

"Hagan's Lace," Quickdraw murmured from beside them. "I'd bet my truck you could give some of those Hagan bulls a run for their money."

"She's really okay?" she asked, and he could tell she still had that lingering insecurity and needed reassurance. Sweet Raven.

"She's a badass," Dead rumbled, squeezing her shoulders.

"Hagan's Lace," she repeated in a whisper. The black was fading from her eyes as she searched Dead's face. "I like that."

THIRTEEN

"What kind of grown man drinks Capri Suns?" Two Shots asked Dead.

Dead didn't answer. He just looked Two Shots dead in the eyes as he drained the package of sugary beverage.

He sighed loudly and pointed to Raven sitting on the fence next to him. "You can't question my manhood, Moo Shots. I got a Hagan riding shotgun." He grinned. "Shotgun is what I named my dick."

"Dude!" Two Shots groused as Raven and Cheyenne cackled.

Even Quickdraw pursed his lips against a smile, and that one never smiled.

Raven was settling into man-banter better. She

had Dead to thank for that. He was the king of the one-liners. She appreciated his talent in verbal sparring. Like right now? She was barely even blushing.

Cheyenne was standing below them, typing away on her phone. "What are you up to, boss lady?" Dead asked. "You been ignoring all this intelligent conversation to stare at your phone. You know, cell phones can become an addiction. Do we need to have an intervention?"

Cheyenne didn't even look up from it as she muttered, "Your conversations are never intelligent, and I can multitask. I've heard every dumb thing you boys have said. I'm editing pictures and talking to Tommy."

"Tommy who?" Two Shots asked. "We know, like, eight Tommys."

"Tommy Hane. You know, I'm just texting with the organizer of the whole Pro Bull Shifter Riding Circuit. No big deal."

"My baby's a *business*woman," Two Shot's said proudly from where he was leaning on the fence next to his mate.

Cheyenne snickered. "All three of y'all are about

to be real happy I'm working right now."

"Oh, yeah?" Quickdraw said. "And why's that?"

Cheyenne finally looked up at them. "Go check your bank accounts, boys. Y'all are welcome."

Dead, Two Shots, and Quickdraw all wore matching expressions of utter confusion as they pulled their phones out of their back pockets.

Quickdraw was apparently the quickest at getting into his online banking. "Holy shit," he muttered, his dark eyes going wide as he stared at his phone. "I'm getting a bigger camper than Dead." He walked off and whooped. Loud enough to echo through the clearing, he repeated, "I'm getting a bigger camper than Dead!"

"I can't remember my dang password!" Dead complained. He stared off into space with a frown and a faraway look. "Is it turtlepoops69 or bigdonglongschlong123?"

"You're ridiculous, man," Two Shots muttered. "Why is my internet so much slower than Quickdraws...? Wait! Okay, I'm in and, holy hell!" He jerked his attention to Cheyenne. "What did you do?"

"I've been in negotiations for bigger money for wins. The riders' incomes were so unbalanced to yours, and now that the PBSRC is getting that huge pay boost with the public jumping on board, there was money to allocate. I went to battle fighting for the bulls to get a pay jump if they end up in those tops spots."

"This is more than I was making in a year!" Quickdraw yelled. "On one event!"

"Oh, it's turtlepoops69," Dead murmured. "Oh. My. Balls." He lifted his stunned gaze to Cheyenne. "Is this for real?"

"Yep. Been working on it for the last few weeks. I even hired a lawyer to negotiate new payment for you boys, but I kept it quiet just in case nothing was fixed. I found out the pay scale changed right before the last event but I wanted to surprise you! I wanted you to see the change in your pay when it hit your accounts."

"You're a mother-freakin' superhero, Cheyenne," Dead murmured. "This makes a huge difference."

Dead dragged his gaze to Raven, who was beaming so big her face hurt. "Congratulations!" she squeaked out, shaking his arm. "You got a pay raise!"

"And it'll stay raised so long as you stay in the top ten bulls. Top three gets those huge payments, though, and whoever ends up first in the entire Battle of the Bulls circuit is going to get paid a stupid amount of money."

"How much?" Quickdraw asked, pacing back to them.

"On top of what you make in each event…" Cheyenne bit her lip, building up anticipation.

"Woman, spit it out!" Dead yelped.

"Number one spot gets half a million dollars. Two gets two-hundred-fifty thousand. Three gets a hundred thousand. The circuit is matching shifter payouts to the rider's payouts."

Quickdraw and Two Shots screamed and threw their cowboy hats into the air. And now they were holding each other's arms, yelling in each other's face, hopping around in circles with each other like weirdos.

But Dead was quiet, and trouble swirled in his eyes. "They really have that much money to allocate to the bulls?"

"Dead, you don't understand how much attention the circuit, and you boys, are getting right now. You're the draw. Without you powerhouse bull shifters, there is no circuit. This is a way to get the competition between all of you ramped up, too, and that's what the audience wants to see. Y'all ain't battling it out over chump change anymore. It's big money, and you'll have every bucking bull shifter gunning for you."

"That's what I'm afraid of," Dead said softly.

Quickdraw stopped jumping around like a lunatic. "You scared of a little competition?"

"No. I'm scared of what people will do to compete. The most influential color in the world is green."

Quickdraw frowned at him, and Two Shots shook his head at Dead. "What do you mean?"

Dead hopped off the fence and reached up for Raven's waist to help her down. "It's the color of money. Forget it. Today is a good day. We're rich, let's go celebrate."

Raven rested her hands on his shoulders and slid off the fence, and as she parted her lips to ask if he was okay, Dead turned around with a too-bright smile. "I'm taking this heifer on a shopping spree in town. We'll meet you at the campground tonight."

"Where are you shopping?" Quickdraw asked.

"I promised this pretty lady a new pair of boots, ya stage-five clinger."

Quickdraw crossed his arms over his chest and looked at the ground. "I was just asking so we know where you are, so we can make sure you're safe. It's good to tell your herd where you are."

"You want to hug goodbye?" Dead asked, veering toward Quickdraw with his arms out.

"Fuck off. I was trying to be nice."

"Well, cut it out," Dead muttered. "It's weird. You can't split my lip," he said, pointing to the half-healed gash in his bottom lip, "and then be nice to me. It plays with my emotions."

Cheyenne and Two Shots were chuckling.

"Whatever," Quickdraw muttered, then made his way toward his truck. "See you assholes when I see you. Die or don't die, doesn't make any difference to me."

"Awww, you big teddy bear," Cheyenne called. "You wuv us."

Quickdraw threw a grossed-out look over his shoulder. "Break all your hips."

Raven's chest was full of happiness and laughter as she climbed in the passenger's seat of Dead's truck.

"I changed," she blurted out as he buckled his seatbelt.

"You sure did."

"I mean I changed in front of people. And I didn't break all the fences!"

Dead snorted. "Well, we're gonna have to send this ranch a check for the cost of a gate, but no, you didn't break all the fences." He turned in his seat and leaned on the console, studied her face. "You were so goddamn beautiful out there."

Her whole torso filled with relief. "Really?"

Dead just shook his head back and forth. "I've never seen anything like you. That beast is inside of such a sweet soul. You're perfect just how you are, Raven."

Her smile couldn't physically get any bigger.

"Except for one thing," he amended.

She danced in the seat. "What one thing?"

"Girl, you could wear the hell out of some boots. You earned 'em in that arena. You don't realize it yet, but you're cowgirl AF. That's the biggest compliment I can give you."

She wiggled her hips again in a little happy dance and said, "Thank you." Then she buckled her seatbelt and chattered to him about all the things she felt when she was changing into her cow...into Hagan's

Lace.

All the way to town, he kept his hand resting on her thigh, and for her, it made her feel so comfortable. It made her feel safe and secure and confident. He really wasn't running from her animal. Now? He'd seen her at her worst, but was looking at her like that wasn't the worst at all. Like maybe that side of her was good.

He pulled his truck into a parking lot for Hoodie's Saddle Shop, parked across several parking spaces in the back with the camper, and told her, "Wait there. I'll get your door."

Her stomach leapt around as she watched him jog around the front of the truck. He pulled her door open and held his hand out for her.

Raven slid her palm against his. So warm. So strong. She clutched her purse with her other hand and slipped out of the cab of his truck. She gave a shy smile to the ground when he intertwined their fingers, held her hand firmly, and led her into the store.

Hoodie's didn't just sell saddles as the name implied. It sold lots of things.

Wide-eyed, Raven looked around the shop, from

the glass case of belt-buckles, to the racks of clothes, to the shelves of bolo ties and cowboy hats, to the rows and rows of cowboy boots in the back.

"I don't think this place is my style," she whispered.

"Trust me," Dead said, bumping her shoulder. "I won't make you compromise your style."

"Okay. Where do we go first?"

"We're workin' from the bottom, girl. Boots first." Dead pulled her hand and lead her toward the stacked shelves of boots. The smell of leather was heavy in the air, and Raven brushed her fingers across the row of boots they walked down.

"What size?" he asked.

"I'm a seven."

Dead twisted and gave her a wink. "Nah, you're a straight ten, but a size seven shoe."

That boy would make her blush her whole life. She was calling it. "You're smooth."

"Yeah, well, I wasn't always so suave." Dead sat her down on a bench and grabbed a few pairs of dark leather boots. "I had braces when I was in high school. And I had a little extra cushion for the pushin'. And I was awkward with every girl because I'd been raised in my older years by my dad, who was also not so smooth with women."

"You were chunky?" she asked him.

"Oh, yeah, I ate like a cow when I was a kid."

"Meee tooooo," she sang out. "Maybe that's a cow shifter thing then. I wonder if Two Shots and Quickdraw went through the same when they were kids. My friend Annabelle never gained an ounce, but she's a werewolf. They have ridiculous metabolisms."

She pulled on the first boot and stood, looked in the full-length mirror on the wall. "Hmmm. I like it, but let me try on the plain black one."

A saleswoman was organizing a rack of boots. She turned to them and said, "You like the black ones? Do you have a preference in what it's made of?"

"Oh, no. I don't really know anything about these kinds of boots."

"Why?" Dead asked. "Whatcha got?"

The sales lady, Linda, her nametag read, got a conspiratorial grin. "I have a pair of Lucchese boots saved for the last couple of weeks, but I won't be able to come up with the money for them. They happen to be size sevens like you're looking at."

Dead lifted his chin and cocked an eyebrow.

"What are they made out of?"

Linda's grin grew bigger. "Python."

"Oooooh," Dead drawled. "Yeah, she needs to see those bad boys."

"But I feel bad," Raven said. "If I like them, I'll be taking the boots you wanted."

The woman waved her off. "I have nineteen pairs of boots. I won't starve for them."

She was gone and back in a jiffy with a box. Linda and Dead stood there with an air of anticipation as Raven pulled back the thin tissue paper printed with the boot logo.

Whoa. She pulled one out of the box in awe.

They were tall but fitted at the ankle, jet black like her cow, and had a good heel.

She looked at Dead.

"They feel important to me, too," he murmured. "Put them on."

In a rush, she pulled off her motorcycle boot and pulled on the other. It fit like a glove. But when she took the second out of the wrapping, she caught a glimpse of the price tag.

"Dead, these are way too expensive!"

He looked at the price tag but didn't seem

surprised in the slightest. "Every good woman deserves a good pair of boots."

"But—but—"

"Try the other on and let me see you catwalk them."

"Okay," she uttered on a breath. She pulled the other one on and stood. They were comfortable and hugged her ankles and calves just right.

The look on Dead's face drew her up short. The smile had slipped from his lips, and his eyes were full of intensity as he dragged his gaze up and down her body, to the boots and back up to her eyes. "Go look in the mirror," he said low.

She made her way to the full-length and gasped. She turned to the side and propped one up on the toe. The heels on these and the shape of them made her legs look long and slender. She was wearing ripped-up black shorts, another ripped-up tank top Dead had made, and her hair was hanging down in dark waves. She'd never thought in a hundred years she would ever be caught dead in a pair of cowboy boots, but these were so badass.

But...

"They're so much, though."

"Will you wear them?" Dead asked softly.

"For this much money? I'll wear the freaking soles off them."

He chuckled a deep, rich, warm sound. "Then those are the ones."

When she turned around, he was taking a picture of her. "I'm sending this to the herd."

"Okay, wait, let me pose!" She grabbed a black cowgirl hat off the display near her and put her hand on her hip and smiled big.

Dead took a picture and then told Linda, "I think she needs a hat, too. That one's loose. Do you have more of those in a smaller size?"

"The hat?" Raven asked. She removed it from her head and studied it. The felt hat was pure black with a black braided piece of leather and a black feather. "Is this a raven's feather?" she asked Linda.

"It sure is. And I think we have a couple more. Let me check the sizes on them." She bustled away toward the wall of hats.

"I think this is the first time I've ever had a boner in a western shop," he admitted in a whisper.

She looked down and, yep, he sure did.

She laughed and handed him her hat. "Want to

cover it?"

"I just have to think of something unsexy. Definitely not you in short shorts, boots, and a hat."

"How about hugging Quickdraw."

"Oh, yeah. Yep. Yeah, that's working."

"I have a six and three quarter. Let's see if this one fits," Linda said, handing her a raven-feather hat.

Raven slid it over her head. It was snug, but not too tight, just firm enough not to fly off easily in a stiff wind. "Wait, let me check the price—"

"No!" Dead said. "You're ruining the game. This is a shopping spree."

"Well, you haven't gotten anything yet."

"Girl, don't test me. I will buy three belt buckles with longhorns on them before you can take a piddle."

"Can I pick stuff out for you?" she asked.

"Hell, yes. Dress me sexy!"

Linda laughed and told them they were funny. Raven spent the next twenty minutes picking out a black button-down shirt, dark-wash Wranglers, and a black belt buckle with—you guessed it—a longhorn on it.

"I think you should wear this all the time," she

said, patting the belt buckle as Linda rang them up. "The cow looks like me."

"Possessive woman. You just want me wearin' your picture over my dick."

"You're Dead of Winter, aren't you?" the Linda asked.

Dead looked startled but recovered fast enough. "I sure am."

"Um, can we get your autograph?"

"We?" he asked.

"Me and all my co-workers." Linda gestured to a trio of ladies behind a rack of leather wallets, trying to look busy. "We were trying to figure out if it was really you."

"Oh, hell yeah, we can take a picture."

"I can take it for you," Raven offered.

"Really?" Linda asked.

"Oh, absolutely." Raven took her phone and waited for all the workers to pile in beside Dead for a picture. She clicked the photo a few times, just in case anyone blinked, and handed it back to her.

"Is this the girl on your Instagram page?" Linda asked, gesturing to Raven.

"Me?" Raven asked, pointing to her chest.

"Hagan's Lace," Linda said, aiming the phone at her.

Sure enough, she had Dead's Instagram pulled up where there was a picture split in half. On the left side, it was her face, speckled with mud, a slight frown furrowing her dark brows as she looked at the camera. In the other, it was her animal, looking straight at the camera with fury in her eyes. The spliced picture was all gritty. She looked like a half human-half animal monster.

The caption read, *I run with beasts. #HagansLace #MooCrew #Lubbock #sheiscomingforyou*

"When did Cheyenne even take those?" she whispered. "That's a picture of my animal." She pulled a face at Dead and repeated it, "That's a picture of my animal. For the world to see. On a page with"—she checked his follower count—"a million followers! Is this okay?"

Dead was grinning at the picture and nodding his head. "It's more than okay. People should see her. They should see you."

Her mind was spinning as Dead finished paying for all their wares, and as they walked toward the door, he threw his arm around her and drew her in close, kissed the side of her head. "Are you overthinking it?"

"Of course."

"That picture is you, Raven. Own it."

"But Cheyenne put it on your page. You have so many followers who will see it."

"So? I'm proud of you. That picture belongs there."

And that was what Dead did. He made things okay. He settled her. He rolled with the punches and never, ever, made her feel hidden.

That man made her feel comfortable in her own skin, whether woman or beast.

The second she made it through the door Dead held open for her, she pranced. Pranced! Because she got her some new boots, and there was something magical about having a brand-new pair of boots to break in. She squeaked and jumped around him as he laughed and tucked the bags closer to his sides so she didn't knock them.

"Cow shifter named Raven raised by humans who hops like a bunny."

"Thank you thank you thank you!" she crowed.

"I'll make you a deal."

Raven peeked in the biggest bag and pulled out the boot box. "Whatever it is, my answer is yes."

"In that case, we doin' doggy style toniiiight."

Raven cackled. "I'm in."

"Technically speaking, I would be in. You. I'm in you. Get it?"

"Perv joke," she called and offered him her knuckles to bump, which he did.

"Are you going to put them on right here in the middle of the parking lot?" he asked.

Indeed, Raven was squatted down, pulling the gorgeous boots from the box. Her butt cheeks were probably hanging out of her short shorts.

"Your ass looks really good right now," Dead murmured, and when she looked up, his eyes were glazed over as he stared.

Raven waggled her eyebrows at him over her shoulder. "Did I just put you in a booty trance?" she asked, bouncing it a little.

"You did indeed," he whispered.

An older lady with gray bouffant hair, a western print button-up dress, and some brown boots walked past them through the parking lot and said, "Uh, uh, uh. You young'uns are too much these days."

"Sorry!" Raven called.

"She ain't sorry," Dead called after her. "I'm always trying to get her to stop being so scandalous because I'm a gentleman, but she's just built like this."

The lady disappeared into the store, but Raven could've sworn she said the word "floozie" under her breath. Cow shifter hearing was very good.

It probably had looked like she was twerking in the parking lot but, pish posh applesauce, none of that mattered to her right now because she had in her hands on a pair of the finest boots she could ever imagine.

"If I were Cinderella, I would wear these to the ball instead of glass slippers."

"Expensive shoes to lose."

"I wouldn't lose them. Prince Charming would just never find me."

"Oh, I would find you," he growled.

The grit in his voice made her stop pulling her motorcycle boots off her feet and look up at him. His eyes sparked with intensity, and his smile belonged to a wolf.

"I have an admission," she murmured, ducking her eyes before she chickened out of saying this.

"Lay it on me."

The fine leather creaked softly as she slid on the boots. "I think you're very very handsome."

"And?"

"Are you fishing for more compliments?"

"Hell, yeah, I love compliments."

"And you're kind, patient, and you don't make me feel less than you just because I'm a girl."

"Why would I do that?" he asked, a frown drawing his eyebrows down as he knelt beside her.

"Because you're a big, badass bull shifter who has this amazing job and all these fans and your animal is just a monster in the best of ways. And I'm a cow shifter."

Dead rolled his eyes. "Cow shifters are the shit. You know how hard it is to find one of you? You're like a goddang unicorn. Look." He held up his phone in front of her. Already there were 2400 likes and 169 comments on the pictures of her that Cheyenne had posted.

"And look at this asshole." He pointed out the last comment.

Atta boy, but also knock her up quick before she figures out you're a turd. That's quite a lady. Trap her fast. Love you, boy.

It was from a commenter named LuckyBeast.

"That's my old man, telling me to trap you."

She belted out a laugh and read it again. "Oh, my gosh, that's your dad? Okay, he sounds funny."

Dead clicked his tongue behind his teeth and shoved his phone into his back pocket. "He thinks he is. We've gotten off track. Back to the deal I'm gonna make you."

"Oh, yeah, I forgot." Raven stood and stretched her leg out, posing for him as he shoved the box back into the big bag. "What's the deal?"

He pulled the black cowgirl hat out of the other bag and slipped it onto her head. "You wear your new boots and hat to the rodeo this weekend, and I'll wear the outfit you picked for me in the interviews."

"Really?" she asked in a higher pitch than she'd intended.

Dead swatted her on the butt as they started walking toward the truck again. Raven was back to prancing around—because new boots.

"Really, really. I don't think I've ever worn all black or dressed up before. Sometimes I don't even put a shirt on for interviews."

She laughed and opened the back door for him to put the bags inside. "And that's probably why ninety-nine percent of your fans are of the female variety."

"So you're saying I look sexy with a shirt off," he said as he led her around the truck.

Dead opened her door and helped her in. Dang, this thing was lifted high off the ground. As she buckled, she spouted off, "And you have great hair and a great beard and I love your tattoo, and your smile makes me blush lots, and I like the way you look at me, and the way you talked to my parents like you've known them for years, and the way you drive when you're muddin', and how comfortable you make me, and how much fun you are, and your jokes make me laugh, and you radiate positive energy, and it's impossible for anyone to be in a bad mood around you."

"I put Cheyenne in a bad mood all the time," he teased.

"It's impossible for anyone but Cheyenne to be in a bad moooooood around you." She grinned brightly. "Cow joke."

"Perfectly executed," Dead told her with a nod.

They grabbed lunch at a drive-thru fried chicken

joint and made another four-hour trek toward a park the next state over where they were supposed to stay the night. They filled every one of those hours with a constant, easy chatter. Sometimes it was joking and lighthearted, and sometimes they talked about the real stuff. Their pasts and childhoods, triumphs and losses. And sometimes a song Dead liked came on the country station, and he would turn it up and sing along, his hand resting easily on her thigh or holding her hand.

He had a great on-pitch baritone voice that she loved listening to. And plus, he sang with a smile on his lips, so she got a little awed when he sang along with the radio. She wasn't much of a singer herself, but she liked seeing all the different layers and hidden talents Dead possessed and the world didn't even know about. Just her.

This felt...right.

If someone looked at them, the cowboy and the tattooed rocker, perhaps Raven and Dead didn't look like a match. But they were in surprising ways. She'd never felt so at-ease, or like she knew someone so well so soon. It was her tendency to open up slowly. Painfully slowly sometimes, and it had always made it difficult to make new friends or hold relationships.

That had been a source of insecurity, but maybe, just maybe, she'd been waiting for someone like Dead to come and open her up.

No, it didn't matter what they looked like or what people thought of them.

They matched just fine.

FOURTEEN

Lubbock, Texas. There wasn't a lot here for the casual tourist, but the rodeo arena was a sight to see.

Why was Raven so nervous?

Raven wrung her hands and paced near the viewing pens. Dead had changed, and crowds of people were drifting around looking at the bulls.

"I don't really like this part either," Cheyenne said from beside her.

"Yeah, my animal would break down all those fences and ruin everyone's life."

Two Shots' huge white bull slammed his head against the gate when a couple of riders got too close.

"Hey!" Cheyenne yelled, charging them. "Get away from him."

"We didn't even do anything," one of them said, but the cruelness in his eyes said that was a lie.

"Whatever you're saying to him, fuck off." Cheyenne shoved one of them hard, and he threw up his arms in surrender. He walked away slowly, muttering a whole string of somethings that pissed Raven off.

"Jackasses," Cheyenne muttered as she posted up in front of her mate's pen.

Dead was in the biggest pen, trotting back and forth along the back fence, clearly agitated. He hated humans so much.

"Everyone start clearing out and find your seats!" one of the handlers announced.

This was a humongous arena, even bigger than the last one. The dirt arena was surrounded by fencing covered in brightly colored sponsor signs. The fencing was all burgundy to match the rows of seats that encircled the arena. There was a small chute on one side that Cheyenne had explained was for the roping events, and on this side were six bucking chutes.

Workers and organizers, riders, announcers, and fans were all buzzing around like bees. Back behind the chutes, where the crowd couldn't see, was where they were now. There were tons of pens stretching as far as she could see, and a maze of alleyways and swinging gates. Everything and everyone had a purpose here, and it was running like a well-oiled machine. She mostly stayed out of the way and invisible—her comfort zone.

"My hat's not on backwards, is it?" she asked Cheyenne.

Cheyenne stopped glaring at a group of riders walking past long enough to check her out. "Nope, it's on just right."

"First bull is hitting the alley!" a handler called, and any stragglers hustled out of the narrow space that led back to a row of changing rooms. Each bull shifter had their own.

Raven climbed up the fence with Cheyenne and watched as Quickdraw trotted past. He veered off at the last second and slammed his horns into a fence the riders were sitting on top of.

Raven giggled and so did Cheyenne. "There's a hundred percent chance he finds those idiots before he bucks and fights them. He acts tough, but he's protective of Dead and Two Shots."

Four more monstrous bulls trotted by, one at a time, each being herded into separate rooms and the doors closed behind them.

Dead was next, and Raven didn't even think about it. She just jumped down to go with him as his massive black and white bull came charging out of his pen and into the alley.

"Lady!" a handler yelled. "Get out of there!"

For a second, his concern scared her, but Dead slowed to a trot as he approached, and then to a walk as he made his way beside her.

"He hates humans," Raven called over her shoulder. "I'm not that."

"Yeeeaaah!" Cheyenne yelled, and then a shrill whistle sounded.

Okay, she'd really just owned what she was.

"Are you Hagan's Lace," a barrel racer asked from atop the fence as they walked by.

Dead, Dead, he tossed his head and nearly clipped her with a horn. He veered toward her, and Raven had to shove him back onto his path before she got pinned against the fencing. "Yes, I'm her."

"Good to meet you!" the nice woman called.

Chest filling with surprised happiness, she called

out, "Same! Good to meet you too!"

Others murmured as they passed, but she just kept her hand on his muscular shoulder as they made their way to the room with the open door.

"She's really in there with him, and she ain't dead yet."

"Dead, Dead, he'll get her bred," a cowboy snickered to his buddies.

When she rolled her eyes, she caught a glimpse of a television that had been mounted above the alley. She was on there. On TV. Just a girl walking down an alley with her boots and cowgirl hat and a pair of black ripped wrangler shorts, her hand resting on the shoulder of a horrifically oversize black-and-white bull. His tail twitched with every step.

Startled by the TV, Raven turned back around and, sure enough, there was a camera man kneeling down at the other end of the alleyway, camera pointed right at her.

Geez, her life was so strange now. Not sure how to handle it all, she smiled, gave a little wave, and said, "Hi!" loud enough to be heard over the buzz and bass of the announcer speaking to the crowd in the arena.

Cheyenne was smiling so big, her whole face was involved, but Raven couldn't figure out why. She just followed Dead into his changing room and closed the door behind them. By the time the door clicked closed and she'd turned around, Dead was already in his human skin again and standing to his full height.

God, he looked good—all flushed from his change, his perfectly defined chest and abs flexing with his breath. His fists were clenched at his sides, his powerful legs splayed, and his darkened eyes were roiling with intensity. His smile was slow but easy, and as she made her way to him, the tension left his body little by little. By the time she pulled off her hat and slipped her arms around his waist, his rigid body had gone soft for her.

It felt so good to just rest her cheek against his chest and melt into his touch. He rubbed her back and laid his head on the top of hers.

"Hey, Raven?"

She just knew he would say something so romantic in this moment. Just knew it. She smiled mushily and asked, "Yes?"

"I think all of the girl vitamins are out of my system."

With a frown at the wall, she asked, "What?"

"And today is the day," he said mysteriously.

Raven leaned back and stared up at him. "What is today?"

"The day I allow a female to dictate how my beard is trimmed."

Raven parted her lips to ask questions, but closed them again when she realized she didn't even understand enough to ask a good question.

"I'm abiding by the contract. Cheyenne wins. I figure it's the least I can do since she works so hard to make my life easier." He nodded magnanimously. "I accept your proposal, Raven."

"Proposal?"

"My answer is yes. I will marry you."

She was pretty sure she could catch a fly with her mouth hanging this far open.

"Just kidding, I know you haven't proposed yet. I give it another week. I want white gold for my ring." He laughed at his own jokes. "I mean your proposal to cut my hair and trim my beard and make me into a ten."

"You're already a ten, Dead."

"Mmmmm. I'm a nine point nine. There's room

for improvement." He released her and made his way to a duffle bag full of what appeared to be power drinks, beer, his flank rope, and a hair trimming kit, which he pulled out and held up like the monkey with the baby lion in the *Lion King*. "Make me into a ten."

She giggled and shook her head. "You're so weird."

"Yes, but there is a reason for my weirdness tonight. Want to know what it is? Huh? Huuuuuh?" He pulled on a pair of jeans. "I'll give you some hints. Planes, good seats, yo momma, good first impressions, and a midnight boner."

"Is this a riddle? I'm very bad at riddles."

"Facetime your mom."

Feeling like a whale out of water, she pulled her phone from her back pocket and dialed her mom. As it rang, she whispered, "Am I really supposed to be the one to propose?"

He grinned. "I will be a groomzilla."

"Hellooooo!" Mom answered over the noise of a crowd.

"Dead said to call you and...wait—" She squinted as her mom panned her phone around the familiar looking arena. "Are you here? In Lubbock?"

"Yes!" She aimed the camera at Dad and Annabelle, who were waving from some very impressive seats. "Dead got us front row tickets!"

Annabelle leaned into the frame with mom. "And there's a seat for you, too! He got us flights here!"

Mom chimed in, "And he's taking us to dinner after his interviews! *And* he got us VIP passes! And—"

"Oh, my gosh, you're really here!" Raven yelped. "My favorite people are here! Dead!" She offered him a wide-eyed look. "You brought my favorite people here!"

His smile was all mushy as he sat on the bench and pulled her onto his lap. She kept the camera angled at their faces. "Do you like the seats?" he asked Mom.

It was Dad who answered from the row above them. He was sitting next to a tall man in a cowboy hat. "You can't get any better seats than these! We are right by the chutes! Your dad has been explaining everything to us!"

"Hey, Dad," Dead said as the old cowboy tossed them a wave.

"That's your dad?" Raven asked, completely stunned. "Hi, Mr. Dead. Mr. Winter? It's so nice to meet you! I'll come out and shake your hand as soon as Dead heads up to the chutes!"

Dead's dad gave a chuckle and nodded. "Can't wait to meet the lady behind that Hagan Heifer. Knew it would take someone special to get to Dead." His voice was all gritty and had a deep southern accent.

"Okay, you wild things, I have a round of beers and hot dogs coming up to you any second now," Dead told them. "I'm gonna get my head in the game, and me and the herd will hopefully put on a good show for you tonight."

"Good luck!" Mom called.

"You're going to do great!" Annabelle cheered from beside Mom.

"Are you wearing Team Dead shirts?" Raven asked, narrowing her eyes at the logos on Mom and Annabelle's T-shirts.

"Oh, yeah, Dead had these waiting at will-call with our tickets," Annabelle explained, pointing to the *Dead is the horniest* logo with a cartoon rendering of Dead's bull, horns bigger than real life.

It was a ridiculous shirt. It was so…so…Dead.

"Oh, Lord," she muttered through her giggling.

They said their goodbyes and hung up, and she

immediately turned around and straddled Dead's lap. She hugged him as tight as she could and blinked hard against the tears building in her eyes. "You do the best surprises. You think of everything."

"Are you happy?" he asked.

"You know I am."

He swallowed hard. "Yeah, but I like hearing you say it."

"Dead of Winter," she murmured, easing back to cup his face. She locked her gaze on his so he could see how truthful her words were. "You make me so happy."

"I like that," he said. "I like it more than I've maybe liked anything in my life."

"Now," she told him, trying to look stern, if one could even look stern with tears in her eyes. "You have a rider to buck off. You have work to do. You have a rank to fight for. It's all up to you how tonight goes. How is your shoulder?" she asked of his sore arm. He'd hurt it a couple rodeos back and was still recovering.

"Feels good. I feel ready."

"Damn right, you're ready. How much time do we have?"

"Half an hour. Just enough time for you to keep my mind occupied and cut this mop of hair."

She dismounted him and pulled him over to the small bathroom area near the shower. She placed a plastic chair under him and made him sit. A few test buzzes of the trimmer and a couple threatening snips of the scissors, and she asked him seriously, "Do you trust me?"

"What's the worst that could happen?"

"Um, I have the guard too low and accidently trim your beard too short and you have to shave the whole thing off."

Dead tensed. "Woman, don't do that. My power is in my beard."

She snickered and told him, "I probably won't let you lose your hair powers. Hold still."

Dead exhaled a nervous sigh and leaned his head back slightly, then closed his eyes. "I mostly trust you."

"I mean, I wouldn't, but you do you," she muttered under her breath as she started trimming his nipple-length beard much shorter.

Raven was quiet while she worked, completely focused. Pantera was playing in the background, and the murmur of the announcer and the crowd outside added to the soundtrack. Dead was buzzing with tension the closer they got to the time.

"Ten minutes," a handler called through the door with a soft knock.

"Yep!" Dead called out, but they didn't even need that much time. Raven was already cleaning up his hair in the back, fading the shorter cut up to the hair she'd left longer on top. She was quick.

"I used to cut my Barbie and Ken dolls' hair," she said. "I also had a Yorkshire Terrier named Frederick for thirteen years, and I did all his grooming, so I'm pretty much an expert. Okay, I'm done."

Dead straightened his spine but kept his eyes closed as she dusted hair off his chest with the flat of her hand.

"You can open your eyes," she enlightened him.

"I'm scared."

"Oh, fuck off, you aren't scared of anything. You're about to buck in front of fifteen thousand people. You're fine."

"Do I look sexy?" His eyes were still closed.

"I'd hit it," she teased.

"That's all I want." He eased an eye open at the

mirror, and then the other. "Holy hell, Raven!" He stood and locked his arms on the sink, turned his face side to side, admiring his reflection. "You've made me into a thirteen."

"Okay, that's a little confident."

"You're right. A fifteen."

She belted out a laugh and put away the trimming kit.

He stood up straight and angled his face. "Do you like it?"

Canting her head, Raven studied him. The beard was only a few inches long now, and she'd faded the sideburns into the short length of his hair. It was longer on top and all mussed from her messing with it.

"I don't think I've ever seen a sexier man in all my life," she answered truthfully.

He parted his lips to say something, but the door swung open and banked against the wall.

Quickdraw was there, his eyes wide, his nostrils flaring. "Something's wrong."

"What?" Dead grabbed her hand and pulled her to the open door as Quickdraw disappeared outside.

Tommy Hanes was a few doors down, yelling into

one of the bull rooms, and a crowd was gathering around it. Down the other end of the alleyway, there was a similar crowd gathered at the last bull changing room.

"Help!" cried a voice in the room beside Dead's room. Dead and Quickdraw rushed to the door.

Quickdraw tested the handle. "Locked."

Dead took one step back and slammed his foot into the door with such force, the barrier shattered inward. Raven followed Quickdraw and Dead into the room and gasped at the man writhing on the floor.

"First Time Train Wreck," Dead murmured, dropping to his knees beside him. The bull shifter was seizing, and Dead took his head in his hands and rested it against his lap. "We're here. We got you." He looked up at Quickdraw. "Call Cheyenne."

"What does she need to bring?"

"The paramedics, and something to pump their stomachs."

"What is it?" the behemoth asked softly as he dialed Cheyenne.

Train Wreck's body relaxed, and he let out a shuddering gasp.

Raven slid to her knees and held his hand.

"They've been drugged. Look at his eyes."

His eyes were focused on Dead, and he was mouthing something, but his pupils were so blown, his eyes only had a thin rim of bright blue.

"It's okay. It's okay," Dead murmured as Quickdraw talked to Cheyenne.

He was trying so bad to say something. Raven leaned closer. "What?"

"Can't...change."

Dead looked like he wanted to puke. "Fuck."

Raven shook her head. She knew what this was. Knew why Dead felt sick. It was Filsa. But why? Money?

"Why weren't you drugged?" she asked. "Why wasn't Quickdraw? Wait, where's Two Shots?"

Seemingly reaching the same thought at the same time, Dead asked low, "Can you go check on him and come right back? I don't want you to see this part anyways. Take Quickdraw. Don't go alone."

"Okay." She stood and bolted for the door, but she couldn't help herself. She turned around right before Quickdraw ushered her out the door. Dead had rolled First Time Train Wreck onto his side and was murmuring something in his ear. Train Wreck was gagging.

She'd never wanted to cry and to kill at the same time. Someone had done something to that man. Someone had done something to at least two more of the bulls, too.

Two Shots. They had to find Two Shots.

"This way," Quickdraw growled, shoving through a crowd to get farther down the hallway to the end rooms.

His shoulders were so wide she couldn't see anything in front of him, and when he stopped abruptly, she ran right into the back of him. He jammed his finger at a group of riders, waiting off to the side. "If you assholes had anything to do with this, I'll fuckin' kill you."

"Why would we?" one of them asked. "We can't win if you don't buck. We didn't do this. We wouldn't."

Raven believed them. They looked as sick as she felt.

"Quickdraw!" a voice echoed over the masses.

"Two Shots! We're here!" Quickdraw pulled Raven in front of him. He swung his massive arm, scooping people out of their way as they headed for the voice.

Cheyenne was with Two Shots, carrying a medical bag. "You didn't eat the snack basket in your rooms, right?"

Quickdraw shook his head. "No. You told us not to eat anything right before we buck unless you give it to us."

"And Dead?" Panic swirled in Cheyenne's eyes.

"He didn't eat anything either," Raven blurted out. "He's okay. Are you okay?" she asked Two Shots.

He looked relieved and shook his head. "I'm fine. Where's Dead?"

"With First Time Train Wreck. He's emptying his stomach."

Cheyenne arched her eyebrows high and her voice was stern as hell as she told them, "I want us all together right now."

As they made their way in Dead's direction, the boys cleared the crowd in front of them. Cheyenne grabbed Raven's hand and squeezed it hard and fast. "Everything's okay." But she sounded just as uncertain as Raven felt.

There was yelling up ahead. Yelling and cussing and the masses were swirling, moving, circling one of the doors.

"Get the fuck out of my way," Dead demanded. He was carrying a man's body like it weighed nothing. The bull shifter in his arms wasn't First Time Train Wreck. This one was blond-headed, and stockier. It must've been another drugged bull shifter Dead was bringing into Train Wreck's room. Dead turned slightly to the side, and Raven caught a glimpse of the man's face. He was foaming at the mouth. Shit.

"You can't just take him," one of the handlers yelled. "The paramedics are coming!"

"Bring me Last Chance!" he yelled at the crowd down the opposite end of the alleyway.

"You shouldn't move their bodies!" an onlooker yelled back.

"Bring me that fuckin' bull, or I will destroy every one of you motherfuckers that gets in my way. We will take care of our own. I don't know who did this, but I know it wasn't me or my herd. Bring Last Chance to Train Wreck's room and make space for the paramedics to get through and work.

Dead cast Quickdraw and Two Shots a fiery look as he disappeared into Train Wreck's room.

"Let's go get Last Chance," Two Shots said low.

Quickdraw and Two headed right for Last Chance's room while Cheyenne pulled Raven inside behind Dead.

Inside the room, Train Wreck was on the ground, covered in towels, his head resting on a duffle bag. He was shivering, but his pupils weren't blown anymore. "They put it in the food," Train Wreck told Raven through chattering teeth. He nodded toward a snack basket that was identical to one that had been sitting in Dead's changing room.

Raven knelt beside him as Dead and Cheyenne went to work on the other bull shifter. They were calling him Jack of All Trades.

Raven murmured to Train Wreck, "I know what this drug is. It's temporary. I know this is awful, but it's temporary. Your bull isn't gone. He's just been put to sleep for a while."

"Whoever did this damn-near overdosed them," Dead growled. "They could've fuckin' killed them." His voice shook with rage.

There was a scuffle outside, and then the sound of chaos followed. Finally, Two Shots came through the door, carrying the body of Last Chance. The bull shifter was seizing in his arms.

"Where's Quickdraw?" Cheyenne asked.

"Fighting."

"Fighting who?" Raven asked.

Somberly, Two Shots answered, "Everyone."

"Why are you helping us?" Train Wreck asked. "We're your competition." He gave a dark huff of a laugh. "You should be happy we're down."

"What an awful way to win," Dead told him as he rolled the bull shifter on his side. "Why would we ever want to win that way. There's no honor in that." Dead flashed him a pissed-off glance. "You're a bull shifter. We don't hate you. We *are* you."

The empty smile fell from Train Wreck's trembling lips. "You're not like I thought."

"Get back!" Quickdraw bellowed, and outside the open doorway, Raven could see the crowd surging forward. The people in front were yelling that Two Shots and Dead were killing the competition.

Idiots. They were trying to save them.

"You and you, come in," Quickdraw yelled, gesturing to someone.

Two paramedics were allowed to pass, and then another two more, dragging stretchers. When they were inside, Quickdraw pulled the door closed.

"Last Chance is the worst," Dead said, pointing to the blond bull shifter Two Shots had brought in. Outside of his seizures, he hadn't moved much.

The next few minutes were chaos. It was Dead putting out orders, Cheyenne working like she knew exactly how to help the paramedics, while Two Shots and Quickdraw went back outside to push back the hoard. Raven did her best to comfort Train Wreck, Jack of All Trades, and Last Chance while the paramedics worked on them.

She'd never felt so worried about strangers in her whole life, but Dead had described how awful the drug was, and she couldn't imagine their fear at the animal disappearing inside of them.

Dead worked relentlessly, reassuring each one, helping however he could. He was magnificent under pressure, but the anger never left his eyes.

"We need room," one of the paramedics said as he rolled Last Chance on the stretcher toward the door.

"We've got you," Dead rumbled and flashed Raven a look right before he disappeared out the door.

He looked gutted with worry.

He and Quickdraw and Two Shots were savage in pushing the crowd back. And to Raven's shock, a few of the other bull shifters joined them, making a pathway for the paramedics to get through. They didn't allow anyone to reach out and touch the bull shifters on the stretchers either. They were like a pack of bodyguards, standing vigilant against anyone who would hurt them or finish the awful job they'd started.

Train Wreck reached out for Dead's arm at the last moment, dragged him beside the stretcher, and Raven could hear him as she followed behind.

"Buck for us tonight. Don't slow down, don't let them win. You go out there and put on a show. Keep that purse big so we have a reason to come back fighting. Swear it."

Dead's eyes were so big as he stared down at the poisoned shifter. He nodded jerkily. "I swear it."

Train Wreck released his wrist and disappeared behind the other stretchers in the crowd.

Tommy Hane came stomping through, looking pissed beyond all measure. "Meeting in the back, now." He jammed a finger toward the end of the alleyway, then turned and cupped his hands around his mouth. "If you are human, not a rider, a handler, or working directly with the organization back here, get the fuck out of my territory. Go find your seats. I need less people here. Bulls and riders, follow me. If you're not in that meeting room in two goddamn minutes, you will not be a part of tonight's event."

Dead slid his hand around Raven's and led her behind Tommy. Cheyenne was on her other side and just shrugged and mouthed, *I don't know* when Raven asked her what was happening.

In the meeting room, bulls and riders filed in and rushed to fill the empty spaces. Tommy kept glancing down at his watch and slammed the door closed after a few minutes.

"Just so everyone is aware, we will be investigating what happened tonight, and when we find out who was involved in hurting our bulls, they will be severely punished. And I'm not talking about human law punishment!" His voice echoed through the room, and his eyes turned the chocolate brown of his animal. "I mean we will punish how we see fit. This poisoning shit will not happen again. It doesn't matter the winnings are bigger now. You will play events fair or you'll be trampled."

"Trampled?" one of the riders asked.

"Did I stutter, Stetson? Welcome to the fuckin' big

league. No more slaps on the wrist. I will put your worthless carcass under one of the bulls you hurt if I ever find out you were involved in hurting them. Is that clear?" His voice cracked with power, and the room delved into complete silence. "A verbal yes is required!"

"Yes!"

"Yes, sir."

"Understood."

"Now, tonight we still have an event to put on. Those people out there paid a lot of money to see this rodeo. Those bull shifters that are going through hell right now wouldn't even want it to be canceled anyway. I know. I asked them. But we are down three bulls right now, and the organizers are scrambling to fill holes in the lineup."

"I'll go twice," Dead offered low. "My second score don't even have to count. I'll go in Train Wreck's spot."

"Perfect. We need some less experienced bulls to fill the other spots. I can see Quickdraw and Two Shots thinking about it, but your bulls are too much for the other riders."

Cheyenne was staring at Raven. Just...staring

from the other side of Two Shots. Obviously staring.

A few loaded seconds passed until another bull shifter raised his hand. "I'll do it, but I need a big rest between. I'm not built like them boys yet." He jerked his chin toward Quickdraw, Dead, and Two Shots. "One buck is hard enough on the body. I need to go first and then last."

"I can work with that," Tommy said. He relayed information into a walkie-talkie and then asked for a last volunteer.

No one was speaking up. No one wanted to do an extra buck, and Raven understood. It wouldn't help their ranks, and it would tire them out. There was the risk of an injury with each professional buck, and if it wasn't for points? It would be tragic to be knocked out that way.

"Hagan's Lace will do it," Dead called out.

"What?" Raven whispered.

Dead lowered his voice and leveled her with a look. "You can do this."

Cheyenne stepped forward, "Tommy, I sent you the video of Raven's cow bucking in practice. She has no experience, has no need for the points, and would be a good match for Buster Jennings."

"I ain't ridin' no cow," Buster yelled.

"Are you scared, you little dipshit?" Dead asked.

"I'm not taking some reject shifter just because the other ones couldn't stop themselves getting poisoned."

Reject. Shifter.

Inside of her, the animal stirred.

Why was Cheyenne smiling at her? "Your eyes look evil as hell right now."

Everyone was chattering and murmuring and pissed off at the audacity of Cheyenne to volunteer a cow shifter, and Raven's fury was growing with each breath as she listened to these idiots.

"I'll do it." She dragged her gaze to Tommy. "I'll buck. Should be easy for tweedle-dickhead over there. I'm just a cow."

"Yeah, it'll be easy, and I won't get no points when you go prissy prancing around the arena with me bored on your back! I'm not getting embarrassed out there!" Buster yelled.

"Then don't get bucked off by a cow, and you won't be embarrassed," Raven barked. "Are we done here?"

Tommy's bushy gray brows were arched high and

his lips were pursed. "I think we have everything we need. Bull shifters"—he cleared his throat and amended—"and cow shifters. I need y'all changed and ready in five minutes. We're going to start loading the chutes. The crowd is already wondering what the hell is going on. And for the love of everything holy, don't eat anything!"

FIFTEEN

"This is really happening." Raven couldn't catch her breath. "I think I'm having a panic attack."

"No, you aren't. You're too badass to panic right now," Dead assured her quietly. "I'm gonna be there to help load you into the chute, and I told Tommy ain't nobody touching your flank strap but me. I won't change and load into my chute until you're done bucking, and at the end of it, Cheyenne will be waiting for you."

"But not where I can get her, right? You told everyone to stay out of my animal's way?"

"Yes, I did. The handlers are professionals at their jobs. No more worrying over the little details. Between me and Quickdraw and Two Shots and

Cheyenne, we've got you."

"What if I kill Buster?"

"Well, good riddance," Dead muttered, pulling her shirt over her head and dropping it in a pile with the jean shorts he'd already peeled off her. "That dude is a chode."

She snorted. She didn't mean to, but it just crawled up her throat and escaped.

Dead gripped her shoulders and lowered down just enough to look at her eye-level. "You're gonna do this, Raven. You're gonna own the animal. You're not gonna hide her anymore, and I'm gonna be so damn proud of you. When that gate opens? You get Buster off you. You put him in the dirt, okay?"

"I can do this," she whispered shakily.

"Louder and like you mean it."

She exhaled and swallowed the coward in her back down. "I can do this."

"Thata girl. Hagan's Lace, go earn that name. Go show people who the fuck she is."

A handler yelled through the door, "We need her now!"

"Quick change, okay?" Dead murmured.

Raven nodded, and he jogged to the door, still

clad in only a pair of jeans. "Do this for them boys that are down right now," he said at the door. He gave her a wink. "I'll see you out there. I'll be with you the whole time."

When he disappeared out the door, Raven clenched her shaking hands. "Be tough. Be the animal. Be tough. Be the animal," she chanted to herself.

The change was painful because she pushed it, but a few moments of bones breaking, skin stretching, fur growing, face elongating, and horns pushing out of her skull, the pain was done, and only a tingling headache was left behind. But that, she didn't care about in this body. All this part of her cared about was filling a bone-deep need for violence. That was the Hagan blood in her. Thanks, Ma. Thanks, Pa.

She charged the door and slammed it open so hard, the thing fell off its hinges. Outside, Dead and a handler were sitting on top of a fence, and Dead was pointing to the rope the handler had just dropped. It had been attached to the door handle. "Told you you wouldn't need that."

The handler looked terrified.

Ima kill him. Teach him real fear. She charged him,

but Dead pulled him off the fence easily. Killjoy.

She tossed him a snort and looked for another victim, preferably one that wasn't under Dead's annoying arm of protection.

There. At the end of the alleyway was a human. Just a little one. Just a man waving a glow stick. Fuck that man. And fuck that glowstick.

Also screw that television above her that showed her trotting down the alleyway. She bucked her back end and kicked up dirt. *Screw you TV.* She pushed her legs and charged toward the man at the end, but he was a smart little cockroach and scrambled over a gate. Oh, another human, another glowstick, and he was in a little pen. She bolted for him, but as soon as she was within killing distance, he slipped through an open gate, and it slammed closed behind him.

Screw you, Billy Buzzkill.

The sting of betrayal was as long as a river and deep as a canyon, and it fueled her rage.

There were people up on the fences of the holding pen now, yelling, pissing her off, and something hit her hind end and stung. A cattle prod? Had someone just hit her with an electric current. Everyone was going to die.

She pushed forward, charging at a man up ahead in the narrowing alleyway. This time, she took matters into her own hooves and jumped for the top of the metal panel to get to him. He yelled and fell backward into the dirt, and she would've cleared it and landed on top of him if someone hadn't used the cattle prod on her shoulder right at that moment. She clattered back to earth and bellowed a battle cry. The panels were closing in behind her, and she had to turn her head to fit her wide horns through the narrow alleyway. She saw light through the open gates ahead, so she kept moving forward, until suddenly the panel in front of and behind her slammed closed with a resounding *gong*. She butted the one in front of her face and kicked viciously at the one behind her, but those suckers were sturdy.

"That's a cow?" Buster asked from above her on the chute platform. She looked up at him and wished to God she could smile at him from this body.

Her horns made it hard to move, and someone was rubbing a rope on her neck. It pissed her off more. Stop!

The flank strap was around her waist now and Buster was easing his legs over her sides. She bucked and kicked, but her horns were between slats of metal in the chute and she was pinned from going anywhere.

Hagan's Lace slammed her side against the chute gate, and Buster cried out but stayed in place. He was messing with another rope on her front end. She hated everything about what was happening. Being trapped. The rope agitating her neck while some cowboy on the other side of the chute panel in front of her rubbed a rope back and forth behind her horns. The rider digging his metal spurs into her ribs. The rope tightening on her front. The rope tightening around her belly. She couldn't see Dead. Dead?

Through the slats, a gateman held a rope taut, waiting to pull the gate open. There were a few bullfighters and some pickup men on horseback on the other side of the brightly lit arena. The crowd was going crazy. Some were booing. Booing? Oooh ho ho ho, she wanted to jump that fence and murder them all.

Open the gate.

"Just stay centered," one of the cowboys advised Buster. "You don't know her bucking style yet, but she ain't gonna have the power behind her, and she should be an easy spinner. Just figure out which way she's leaning, set your seat, and hold on."

"Hagan's Lace." That was Dead's voice.

She twitched her ears back toward him. The song "We Will Rock You" was pounding a bass beat through the whole stadium, rattling her head.

"Don't spin," he told her.

"Fuck you, man," Buster muttered, sitting up farther on his rope hand.

And that was Buster's biggest mistake. It wasn't gouging her with his spurs or calling her names. It was talking to Dead like he was anything less than a king.

Dead told her don't spin? Okay.

"Let's go!" Buster yelled to the gateman.

And then the gate opened.

And for a split second she hesitated in the chute because freedom had come in an instant. She wasn't pinned in place by her horns. She wasn't pinned at all.

She was free to bring hell to earth.

Be the animal.

Don't spin.

SIXTEEN

"Go!" Dead yelled at Hagan's Lace's hesitation.

Her reaction was instant. She yanked her horn out of the slat it had been pinned in and she went straight up and straight out.

When she pushed off the arena dirt and went airborne, time froze. Buster was leaning forward, shoulders tensed, free arm up. Lace's horns were so wide and her shoulders stalky like a bull's. She was meant for this. The cameras were flashing around the arena, the crowd was roaring, and Dead was yelling at the top of his lungs. Cheyenne was screaming beside him, and Buster's team were yelling for him to hold on.

She hit the dirt on her front end, slamming Buster

forward, and that cow didn't go to spinning. She went straight up and twisted instead.

"Oh, my God!" Dead yelled, gripping his hair. He couldn't help his grin as he cheered.

Lace was twisting violently with each buck and Buster was already off balance. She didn't make it a rhythm, never once allowed him to get his seat back before she jerked him the other way.

The announcers were going wild.

The crowd was going wild.

Even the cowboys and riders behind him were cheering.

Lace, with all her ninety-six inches of half white, half black horn, hide all laced with tattoo ink, dark as a demon with a fury to match, was giving one of those rides a cowboy remembered. One that etched into their brains and made them think twice about getting on the back of an animal again.

Lace jumped up in the air again and twisted, kicked her back legs with such power, Buster was flung off her like a rag doll and hit the middle of the arena. She was quick. There were no baby bucks after she flung him. She went straight for him, charging past the bullfighters trying to get her attention.

241

Beside him, Cheyenne gasped and clapped her hands over her mouth.

"She'll pull off," Dead murmured, hoping to God he was right.

Buster was scrambling to get away, trying to get traction in the dirt. A bullfighter ran right in front of Buster, cutting Lace off, and she went for it. She turned and charged him.

The fighter was good as he spun her in a tight circle, but she barely missed him with her horns. Another was right there to pull her away from that fighter, spinning her attention around the other way, and Buster was almost to the rail.

"He's good. He's good," Dead murmured to Cheyenne. "She didn't get him." Thank God. She would've never forgiven herself.

The cheering of the crowd was deafening, and Dead looked over at the VIP box where his dad, her parents, and Annabelle were sitting.

They were all standing, and they were... Going. Wild.

Dead's chest swelled with pride as Hagan's Lace trotted around the outside of the arena. *Go on girl, take that victory lap.* She didn't even realize. She didn't even realize it yet. She was the first cow to ever buck in the PBSRC. She'd just shoved cow shifters onto the map, and she hadn't even meant to. She was just incredible.

Cheyenne squeezed his arm. "Dead, look at the crowd."

Oh, he was. There wasn't a single fan in their seats. They were going insane for Lace.

A pair of pickup men rode behind her, and one of them released her flank strap and herded her toward the open gate in the middle of the bucking chutes.

She was beautiful. Savage. Powerful. Confident. Looking around for a body to fight. Ears erect, head up, horns sharp, black eyes taking in everything. Beautiful badass.

"You're up soon," Cheyenne murmured. "Better go change. There are three other bulls bucking before your first turn."

Two Shots and Quickdraw were already loaded in their chutes and causing chaos as usual. Quickdraw was rattling the chutes with his kicking, and Two Shots jumped and damn near cleared his chute. Good luck to those riders. Those two bulls had just watched Lace kill it, and the momentum was with the bulls now.

As he left the platform, he reveled in the stunned looks the riders were exchanging with each other.

That's right, fellas. My lady is baaaaad.

He'd never been prouder of a ride, and it wasn't even his.

That was love. He wasn't good at romance or feelings, and he'd never been in love before, but this was it. Love was wanting better for your person than you had for yourself. It was contagious smiles, pounding heartbeats, and being there for each other. It was not being scared of the monster in the other person, and oooh, monsters existed in everyone. It was understanding that dark side and caring about the person more for that knowledge.

He loved her. There it was, he loved her, and someday soon, he was going to make it special when he told her. She deserved to feel special.

Because this was it. She was it.

That woman might not know it yet, but she was his.

SEVENTEEN

Raven couldn't stop shaking, but it wasn't from nerves anymore. It was from excitement. From disbelief. From euphoria.

Rushing, she pulled on her Wrangler shorts and shoved her feet into her boots, then placed her black cowboy hat on her head and rushed out of the changing room. When she threw the door open, there was a monster waiting for her. She skidded to a stop and grinned. Her monster.

Dead was changed into his enormous black and white bull, pacing in front of her door.

"I didn't want to miss your bucks," she uttered breathlessly.

His muscles were tensed and he came for her, but

she wasn't scared. He skidded to a stop in front of her and gently bumped her with his head. She hooked her arms under his horns and held his head against hers, then rested her cheek on his forehead for a moment. "You're gonna do this," she gritted out. "You stay in that top three."

She didn't care who was around or who was watching. Dead was hers. She shoved his head back and grinned. "I love you, you big oaf."

His head lifted, his ears twitched and, God, his animal was magnificent. Huge muscular chest and shoulders, big hump of muscle behind his horns. Her animal adored his animal, and that was a first ever. Her animal didn't like anything or anyone...except for Dead.

"Now go to work," she teased. "Momma needs these boots paid off."

"Can you drag him this way?" a handler yelled from by the chutes.

"Yep!" Raven took off jogging, and Dead kept pace with her, trotting with powerful strides. She led him right through the narrowing alleyway and into his chute and climbed out as the handlers began closing him in.

"You're a badass," one of the riders said as she scaled the chute and landed on the platform behind it. He offered his hand for a shake, and she shook it, stunned that he even knew who she was.

"Th-thank you."

"Did you see your score?" Cheyenne exclaimed, running up the platform stairs toward her.

"What score? I thought I wasn't taking a score."

"They gave you one! I negotiated a spot for you here with Tommy right before you bucked! You got a forty-one-point-four on your first buck! Out of forty-five!"

"That's good?"

Cheyenne shook Raven's shoulders and bounced up and down. "Buck, yeah, it's good! I told Tommy I took you on to represent you pro bono, so the circuit wasn't liable if you got hurt. He said if you did bad in front of all those cameras, I was fired, but I wasn't scared for even a second." She knelt down to her bag and handed up a stack of papers. "I need you to sign these real quick if you want to be in the running for money tonight. Let me find that dang pen. It always falls to the bottom," she grumbled as she dug around in her bag.

Raven read the title page.

Bucking Bull Shifter
Seven Day Contract
PBSRC

"You risked your job?" Raven asked her, utterly stunned. "For me?"

"Well, it wasn't really a risk if I knew what was going to happen. Ah ha! Here you go." Cheyenne handed a ballpoint pen up to her. It had a logo with a worm on it.

Raven frowned at it. "What's Willa's Worms?"

Cheyenne shrugged. "I dunno. I like it because the little cartoon worm is cute. I have a few of them. They're my good-luck pens."

Raven skimmed the short contract, only good for this week so she wasn't being locked into bucking for the circuit. She signed it and handed it back to Cheyenne. "Do you mind if I go see my family? Are you okay here by yourself?"

"Oh, yeah, Two Shots already bucked. He's changing, and he'll be here any second. Hey, Raven?"

"Yeah?" she asked.

"Take stock of this moment. You just kept up with bull shifters who have spent their whole lives training for these events. And you did it with no coaching and no prep." She arched her eyebrows. "Your animal is one of a kind."

And for a second, Raven could only stand there in shock. Oh, she knew her animal was one of a kind, but that had never been a compliment until now.

Are you sure you belong here?

That was the question that pretty cowgirl had asked her last week at the rodeo.

Last week, she hadn't known about rodeos or bucking or the work involved behind the scenes. She'd just wanted to meet a bull shifter with a human parent so she could, perhaps, get to understand herself better. Get some answers to the questions that had burned her up all her life. She'd wanted to learn how to control the animal better and hide the animal better, but that's not the lesson Dead and his herd had offered her.

They'd given her something so much better.

They'd taught her to appreciate her animal and, in turn, she appreciated herself more. This was the first time in her life she felt okay. Better than okay.

She felt...normal here.

Are you sure you belong here?

She looked down in Dead's chute as his rider was sliding onto the back of him. She knew how he felt now. Now, she was familiar with the adrenaline, the surge of power, and that pinpoint focus to put a rider in the arena dirt.

Dead, Dead, he twisted his head and looked up at her. Her heart filled with such pride for the man she loved.

She knew this life now. She knew herself. She knew him.

Hell, yeah, she belonged.

EIGHTEEN

Raven tried to sneak up on the VIP box to scare her mom, but Annabelle was facing her way, talking to Dead's dad, and she spied her.

She pitched an excited scream into the universe and caught Raven's hug in the aisle behind their seats.

Annabelle was so ramped up, she jogged in place and squeezed the life out of Raven with her hug, but who needed oxygen anyway? It felt so good to see her and her parents, who were now waiting behind Annabelle to hug her.

She made her rounds and then squared up to Dead's dad, offered her hand. "I'm Raven."

"Girl, you're more than Raven." He jerked his chin

up to the big screen television mounted above the seats on the other side of the arena. It was a slow-motion segment of her ride.

"You're one hell of a shifter, too, Hagan's Lace," he said with a wink.

"Oooooh, that's where Dead gets his charm from. It's from youuuu," she teased.

"Taught that boy everything he knows," he rumbled. "I'm Liam. It's sure good to meet you. Dead has sent me about four hundred texts this week about you. Seems he's a little smitten. And between you and me? That boy don't get attached to people easy. Come on, sit down. We got another round of beers headed our way, and my boy is about to buck."

She took the seat right up front by Annabelle and cheered her brains out as she gripped the railing in front of her.

The announcer's voice echoed through the arena. "Hailing from Montana, he's the baddest of the bad, the maddest of the mad, and has a near-spotless record for throwing riders. I see those signs out there, ladies. I know you showed up for this bull. Takes no shit as a human and murderous as a bull, he's the best of both worlds, but he's got his hands full tonight. For his first ride, Roddy Brander is making a run for a top spot in the Battle of the Bulls events. If he can just hold on for eight seconds and get a score of 80 or better, he can take the lead for the entire circuit. The only thing standing in his way? That bull right there. Y'all lift your glasses. I think they're about ready in the chute..."

The gateman pulled the rope attached to the gate, and the barrier swung open and released hell. That's all she knew how to describe it. Dead studied his rider's strengths and weaknesses before a buck, and was rotating perpendicular high jumps with harsh landings on his front end, then tight spins that thrust his back legs sideways with such force Roddy had trouble finding his balance. And just as he got used to spinning that direction, Dead jerked the other way and flipped Roddy right into the dirt beside him. The bullfighters had to work hard and fast to keep Dead from smashing the downed rider into the dirt, but Roddy scrambled and got to a platform in the middle of the arena.

He screamed a curse that could be heard through the boos and cheers of the arena and tossed his helmet to the ground. One of the pickup men released

Dead from the constraint of the flank strap, and he quit bucking.

Chills rippled up her forearms as Dead trotted around the arena, searching...searching...what was he searching for? Deep down, she knew.

Raven leaned over the railing and took her hat off, waved it. He turned his head and trotted right for her. And when he reached her, she murmured the words she'd first spoken to him, "It's okay." She let a smile take her lips. "Now, go do it again."

Dead blew out an explosive breath and ran for the open gate between the chutes.

A pretty cowgirl with a tray of beers passed them out. "I was told specifically by Dead to make sure y'all aren't thirsty tonight."

"Want to sit with us?" Raven asked.

She laughed as she took their empty plastic cups. "I would love to, but I'm serving all the VIP boxes tonight. We got some bigwigs here watching." She gestured over to a trio of men in clean white cowboy hats, dress shirts and suits, and bolo ties. They were all looking right at Raven so she waved.

They waved right back and gave her nods of respect. One of them gave her a thumbs up and called out, "You had one helluva ride."

Wow.

"You're famous," Annabelle murmured. "Everyone here knows who you are, even when you're in your human skin. And the announcers keep talking about you."

"And look," Mom said, pointing up at the big screen. "They keep replaying your ride between the other bulls bucking."

A black and gray bull exploded out of the chute, and it was exciting to watch, but this bull didn't have as much power in its bucks, and the rider held on for the full eight seconds.

"I never ever would've seen you ending up here," Dad said from behind her.

"At a rodeo? Wearing cowgirl boots and a cowgirl hat?" she joked.

But Dad looked serious, and his gray brows lowered over his glasses. "No, I never imagined I would see the day when you were this happy. And this at ease with yourself. My shy girl. You just went out there and blew me away."

"Blew all of us away," Annabelle agreed.

"Blew this whole arena away," Liam added.

Raven's cheeks were on fire, and she ducked her gaze. Didn't matter how she'd bucked or how confident she was in herself; she would always be shy. It was just a part of who she was. "Aw, I was just stepping in to help out."

"I think that boy is special," Mom murmured. When Raven looked up, her eyes were rimmed with tears. "I always wanted you to find a good match." She pointed to the chutes where Dead was loaded up and causing havoc, slamming his hoof against the back of it. "That's a good match."

And as Raven stood up to watch him buck, anticipating what he would do right along with the rest of the crowd, she thought her mom was right. Who could've matched her animal? Hagan's Lace, as she was now easily calling the beast in her head. Who could've looked at her struggle between woman and beast and understood like Dead? And supported her like Dead? And cared about her perhaps more because the animal existed, not less?

Only Dead.

Before she'd met him, she'd accepted that she would never be quite comfortable in her own skin. It had been a hard thing to come to terms with, but now? She watched him thrashing a rider off his back and then looked around at the cheering arena. He'd brought her to a place where she made sense.

She. Made. Sense.

Because he'd looked at her, taken her under his powerful wing, and told her she made sense. And then he told the whole world she made sense, too.

No one could give her a bigger gift.

She didn't know how she was going to do it, but someday, someway, she was going to repay him.

NINETEEN

This was the part she hadn't mentally prepared for.

In all honesty, she'd forced herself not to think about it—the goodbye.

She broke the heavy silence in the truck. "Where are you heading next?"

Dead reached over and slid his strong hand around hers. "Lincoln, Nebraska."

"Whoo, sounds cold." She shrugged and shook her head. "I don't really know if it's cold there. I've never been. I'm just...small-talking."

"We'll figure things out. I'll be back near Boise in a couple months on another tour stop. I'll swing the herd wide, and we'll spend a couple days near you, okay? I know they'll be okay with the detour."

Her lip trembled so she looked out the window to hide how weak she felt. Two months seemed like an eternity. "I would like that."

His beard tickled her hand as he kissed her knuckles. "You can't take any more time off work?"

She shook her head jerkily. "I already asked Mona. She can't spare me for another week, and I understand. We have a very small staff at the shop. She was already so kind to let me off last minute." That heavy silence was back, the kind that sat on her chest like a fallen tree. "I wish I could stay longer."

Dead didn't answer. Only looked at the airport sign they were driving under and rubbed his cheek on her hand as he held it in place.

"I have plants to water, frozen dinners to eat." She tried joking, wishing she had some magical power to take away the sadness. "And I'll text you a hundred times a day. I really will. I'm a stage-five clinger now. I've learned so much about myself this week, thanks to you."

He chuckled, but the smile that accompanied the rich sound didn't reach his eyes. "I see your parents and Annabelle," he murmured, pulling up to the terminal drop-off.

Annabelle and her parents were waiting by the doors for her and waved when they saw them. Dead parked and hopped out, and as Raven gathered her backpack of clothes she'd collected through the week, they said their goodbyes to Dead. Dad shook his hand and said something low to him, but Raven couldn't make it out over the roaring in her ears.

This was happening. She had to say goodbye to Dead who'd become a comfort blanket for her over the time they'd known each other.

He'd become an anchor. A lighthouse. A protector. Safety. A confidant. A lover and a friend.

To Raven, he'd become crucial.

When she walked away, Dead would stay behind and keep an important piece of her with him—her heart.

She would have to go home without it.

She would have to go home and walk around pretending like it still beat in her chest. Like she was whole when she wasn't and, God, it felt like she'd only just learned how to be whole in the first place.

When Dead turned to help her out of the truck, her parents and Annabelle waved, told her, "We'll meet you inside." They walked through the sliding glass door and disappeared inside the airport.

Dead turned to Raven. "I'll send you pictures of everything we do," he promised, pulling her to him by the hips. "It'll be like you're with us. I'll bring you along."

Thickness in her throat made it impossible to speak, so she nodded.

"You said something last night when I was a bull. Do you remember what you said?"

She'd told him she loved him. Another nod because she couldn't squeeze words up her throat quite yet.

"I've never said it to a woman before, never felt it, and I don't say things I don't mean. I feel it, Raven. I know how important you are." His piercing blue eyes searched her face. "But if I say it now, you'll take it as a goodbye, and that ain't what this is. I'm gonna tell you when I see you next. You understand?"

"You love me?" Her voice shook, and her eyes tingled with welling tears.

He nodded.

"And you'll tell me someday when we see each other again?"

Another nod. "It's a promise."

A promise from an honest man. "That's good enough for me," she whispered.

He leaned down and kissed her. It was one of those kisses that made the whole world fade away. It was his soft fingertips on her cheek, and her hugging his neck so tight. It was up on her tiptoes, their lips saying the words he'd promised her, body melting into body until there was only one of them. It was home.

When a tear fell to her cheek, she broke the kiss, eased down to earth again, and adjusted the strap of her backpack.

"You're important to me, too," she murmured thickly then walked away.

Raven couldn't look back. She couldn't. If she did, she wouldn't be able to do this. She wouldn't be strong enough to.

She knew he waited, though. When she made it to her family inside, she peeked out the window, and his truck was still there. She couldn't see him through the dark tint of his windows, but he'd waited.

Her phone vibrated in her back pocket, so she pulled it out, read the text.

I miss you already.

When she looked up, Dead was driving away with her heart.

What had she been thinking, falling in love with a rodeo man? With a bucker. With a rambler, a traveler, at the mercy of his event schedule but her with roots grown so deep into her hometown.

This was how to rip a person in half. Her family, best friend, job, and home were in one place, and her heart would now be in another. It didn't feel fair.

She was greedy and wanted it all, because how could happiness exist when she was torn in two?

Swallowing down her sadness, Raven sent him a text back.

It's okay. I miss you too.

TWENTY

Three weeks later

"You have three different deliveries in the office," Mona said.

Raven set down the plastic containers of lunch from Sandbox Sandwiches. "Deliveries to take to the funeral home?" she asked, confused. That hadn't been on the schedule this morning.

"No, someone sent you two deliveries."

She grinned and, with a squeak, she ran for the office in the back of the small flower shop. Quick as a whip, she closed the door behind her and bounded over to the desk where there sat a card, a present, and...a bouquet of candies, arranged on sticks like they were flowers. All of her favorite candies were in it, and three packages of Skittles reassured her of who sent them.

She plucked the card off the present and ripped it open in a rush. The card said:

Hey Sexy Heifer,
Five more weeks and your butt cheeks will be in both my hands.
Love and blow jobs,
Dead

So romantic. Her face frozen in a grin, she reached for the other box, but the card beside it fell to the ground, and that definitely wasn't from Dead. The handwriting wasn't familiar. It was loopy and feminine. She knelt and plucked the envelope from the carpet, opened it, and unfolded the handwritten card. There was a black and white picture taped inside of a tall woman holding a baby, and five boys around her of different ages. They all looked somber. Somber and familiar. They all had black eyes. Black eyes just like she got when she was changed or close to a change.

Hagans.

In the background, a man stood stoically. He was tall, intimidating, and impossibly broad-shouldered. There were no smile lines on his face, as if he'd never smiled a day in his life. He was glaring at the woman. Raven looked at the woman's face again, and she could just make out the tears in her eyes.

The letter read:

Dear Raven,

That's what I heard they named you. I wasn't allowed to give you a name. Only a brand, and even that got me in trouble. If they knew what I done with you, trouble wouldn't begin to describe it. But you know what? I watched you the other night on TV. I known it was you. You look like your brothers. Same dark hair, same eyes, same stubborn set to your lips, and that animal inside you is pure Hagan. I watched you on the TV when everyone was away and I cried and cried.

It don't matter what kind of trouble I get into for giving you away, I wanted you to live a better life. I wanted you to live any life. And look at you now. I never been so proud to be a momma as when I was watching you buck.

This will be the last time I contact you, but always always know, you got a fan in me.

Don't look for me. Please. I was supposed to bury you. Stay buried.

No matter what happens, you're worth what I done.

It wasn't signed. Raven read it three times, just bawling as quiet as she could. Someone out there in the world had made a huge sacrifice so that she could be okay.

She took a picture of the card and texted it to Dead while she fell apart propped up against the office desk. A few minutes later, her phone buzzed with his response.

I already know what you're thinking, but you can't look for her, Raven. They'll kill her and come after you. I know this guts you. I wish I was there to hold you and talk you through it. God, I really wish I was. That letter and that picture have to be enough for you. Can I call?

She sniffed and messaged back. *I'll call you when I settle down.* Send.

Yeah, that's what I figured, sweet girl. I'm here. Okay? You aren't alone. I'm here. Always here.

But right now, Dead felt very *very* far away. Too far away.

She reached up to the desk and grabbed the last box. Maybe this was from her biological mother as well. She tore into the paper, ripped off the tape on the box, and opened it to find a book. She frowned. On the cover was a picture of her and Dead. She was walking down the alleyway of the arena away from the camera, human, dressed in her cowgirl boots and hat, her hand resting on the massive shoulder of Dead's bull.

With a soft gasp, she lifted the photobook from the bubble wrap that had protected it and turned to the first page.

A Week to Remember it read, with a picture of her, Dead, and the rest of the herd sitting on a fence at one of the practice bucking chutes they'd stopped at that week. Cheyenne had put her camera on an automatic timer for this picture.

This was from Cheyenne.

Awed, she turned the page over and pressed her hand to her pounding heart as she looked at all the beautiful memories Cheyenne had captured.

A picture of her talking to fans with Dead the first night they met while he signed autographs. He was looking up at her, smiling like she hung the moon.

A picture of them standing under the VIP sign, only inches apart as she looked up into his eyes with raw emotion.

A picture of Raven sitting in the lawn chair by Dead's camper, mid-laugh as he talked to her from where he stood near the grill, flipping a steak.

A picture of her and Dead dancing, Raven's eyes closed, a soft smile on her lips as she rested her cheek against his chest.

A slew of pictures from the day of mudding. One of her through the window of Dead's truck, cracking up right along with Dead. One of Dead carrying her away from the muddy pit that they'd pushed Two Shots' truck out of, both covered in filth. Raven was waving at Cheyenne in that one with a goofy grin on her face.

Had she ever looked so happy in pictures before?

She kept turning the pages and got lost in the memories.

Gas stations. Raven holding two cases of beer in

her hands while she ran to Dead's truck. Practice arenas. A closeup of Dead's hand in her back pocket, cupping her butt while they watched Quickdraw buck. One of her giving him a playful shove and the next of him tossing her over his shoulder. One of Dead leading her into a restaurant, holding her hand.

Three of her laughing with Two Shots and Quickdraw while they were pumping gas into their trucks on opposite sides of the same pump. Pictures of them hanging out in Dead's camper, and then Quickdraw's and Two Shots' campers. One of her and Dead in the buffet line for a little pancake breakfast Cheyenne had made for them.

One of her on Dead's back, riding piggyback style while he talked. By the red in her cheeks, he was probably saying something perverted.

Her first buck in that practice arena. That collage took up a full spread of the book. It was the boys' reactions, the whooping cheers they let off, her mid-flight while she bucked...the pride on Dead's face when she changed back.

Raven was crying again, but this time it wasn't over a broken heart. She was crying because these pictures made her happy down to her soul.

The next pages were of her bucking in the arena. There had to be ten pictures on this spread. It was the sparkles of the camera flashes behind her as she was frozen mid-air, Buster holding on for dear life. One had Dead cheering for her. One was of her family, Annabelle, and Liam in their VIP box, all standing, cheering their guts out for her. Cheyenne had captured her victory laps and Dead's look of utter pride as he stared at Hagan's Lace. She got the scoreboard with her forty-one-point-four. She got the final rankings on the board, Hagan's Lace taking fifth place for that single event. Quickdraw at one, Dead at two, Two Shots at third place.

She'd gotten pictures of them all hanging out with Raven's family and Annabelle afterward, a group photo, all smiles, all genuine happiness.

The last part drew her heart into her throat.

The spread was covered with small, square pictures of Dead. Dozens of them. In each, he was looking down at his phone. It looked like he was texting or checking messages. Her messages. There were a couple of him sitting by himself watching a sunset. The sadness in his eyes in those two photos hurt.

She knew that kind of sadness intimately.

It was hers as well, being away from him.

She turned the page, expecting to find a blank one, and she did. It was blank, but not empty. There was a clear sleeve with a folded letter inside.

Cheyenne wrote:

Dear Raven,

Do you feel it yet? That pull to us? To Dead? Dead told us you haven't been around many shifters like you, so perhaps you haven't put your finger on that feeling yet. That hole. Sometimes herds are formed, and if one goes missing, that hurt is never patched. For us? For three weeks there has been a hole in our herd the size of a bowling ball. It doesn't get better. It gets worse. Dead won't ask you to leave your life if you're happy. He doesn't want to take you away from your family, or from your job, from your best friend or your home. Your happiness means too much for him to ask. So this is me, doing something he did for Two Shots and me once. He took pictures and showed them to us, made us realize what was happening. I hope that's what these pictures do for you.

You belong with us, Raven. Dead is lost without

you. He hasn't told a dick joke in a week. If that isn't a red flag, I don't know what is. And if I'm honest? The rest of us are lost without you too. The boys ask about you every day, and there's this weight on us now as we watch Dead struggle. It's hard to get them to focus on the next event, and the next, when something so pivotal is missing.

Dead misses you.

I miss you.

The boys miss you.

This is me being selfish and asking you to call that place your "old home" and make a "new home" with us.

Dead, Dead, he's in your head, he wants you here with him instead.

You're a part of our herd.

Come home.

Your friend,

Cheyenne

There was a plane ticket resting in the clear pocket. Slowly, Raven pulled it out and read her name across the top. It was for tomorrow morning, landing in St. Louis, Missouri—Dead's next event.

She clutched the ticket and the photobook to her chest and stared at the closed office door.

Cheyenne had titled the book, *A Week to Remember*, but it wasn't just that. It was the week she fell in love, and she'd watched it happen all over again with this beautiful photo collage Cheyenne had taken the time to make for her. It was the week everything had fallen into place and she'd figured out who she was.

That hole Cheyenne had described? She felt it, too.

A herd.

Raven, the reject of the Hagan herd since birth, raised by humans, never quite able to fit in, had somehow secured a place in a real herd with people she adored and a man she absolutely and unconditionally loved.

With a sigh, Raven stood.

Come home.

Tears in her eyes, she nodded.

Okay.

EPILOGUE

Dead fidgeted with his flank strap. The worn thing had lost all of the spiky rope strands and was smooth now with age and use.

Was this worth it?

Was it?

He looked around the changing room. He'd been in thirty others, just like this one. He used to love this. Loved the adrenaline, loved the scent of fur and dominance, loved going after humans, loved the change, loved the bucks. Loved the buzzer that went off *after* a rider's ass had already hit the ground. He'd loved the traveling, loved being around the boys. Loved the recklessness of this life. The chaos and uncertainty of it.

But now?

The arenas were packed now more than ever, but they still felt empty without Raven here to tell him, "It's okay," after he finished a buck. Last week, without her with him, he'd dropped down to fourth place, and this week he needed to get his ranking back and put the herd back together. No pressure or anything.

"Ten minutes," a handler said through the door with a soft knock.

Dead didn't answer, just pulled an energy drink out of his bag. Under it was a package of skittles from his dad and a Snicker's bar from a care package Raven had sent him. She sent one every week. Her favorite candy was Snickers, so she always put one in there for him, knowing his dad had the skittles covered.

Why did his chest always ache so damn bad now?

The handler knocked again.

"Ten minutes, yeah, yeah, I got it," Dead barked out.

When the door creaked open, Dead stood. "I said!—"

Raven popped her head in the door.

Huh. Apparently, energy drinks caused hallucinations these days.

She looked so good right now. Were those black wrangler cut-off shorts? God, his imagination was awesome. Long legs with those badass tattoos, the boots he'd bought her, a blood-red tank top, and her black cowgirl hat. Deeeelicious.

"You owe me an L-word."

Dead frowned. His imaginings weren't usually so demanding.

She cracked a smile.

"Raven?" he asked. God, he was gonna feel dumb if she wasn't real.

She opened the door the rest of the way and blasted her hands on her hips. "I'm prepared to hear it. Lay it on me. Make it mushy."

"Oh, my God, you're really here?" He took a few steps toward her, and then that little hellion closed the gap. She ran to him and jumped, and his dumb ass barely recovered fast enough to catch her.

"Geez, you're heavy, heifer," he joked.

She swatted him and acted offended. "I said be romantic."

He gripped the back of her neck and pulled her in,

kissed the devil out of her. He didn't know about romance-shit, but he did know she always went quiet when he kissed her and always looked drunk afterward. Drunk was probably good.

"Damn, girl, I missed you," he murmured, hugging her so tight. He never wanted her to unwrap her legs from his waist. "When we die, let's die fucking so they can bury us like this," he said.

She tossed her head back with a laugh. "Getting colder. That's not romantic at all."

"What are you doing here?" he asked, swaying them gently.

"I figured out something important while I was trying to make my old life work. While I was trying to love it like I used to before I met you. It didn't work. You know why?"

He shook his head. "Why?"

"Because you are my home, Dead. And our herd is my home. I just needed some time to accept that. We happened fast, and I wanted to make sure this was real for both of us before I left everything behind. So...I left everything to find everything. Do you understand?"

He shook his head in disbelief. "Are you staying

with me?"

"Hashtag camperlife. Hashtag moocrew."

Dead laughed for the first time in what felt like forever. He set her down until her boots were flat on the ground. "You're staying on the tour with me? I just want to hear you say the words."

She cupped his cheeks and searched his eyes. Hers were black right now. Beautiful, badass woman. "Dead of Winter, I'm coming on tour for the rest of the year. And in the offseason, we are going to figure out a home base and a life together. Then next year, we will go on tour again. And again. And again until you don't want to do this anymore. And I'll buck, too. I got paid five thousand dollars when I bucked, and do you know what I did with that money?"

He shook his head.

"I put it in a savings account for a ranch for us someday. For a home. Me and you are gonna build one, okay?"

"Build a life?"

"Yeah," she whispered.

He gripped her hair in the back and tried to be gentle with his next kiss but, goddang, he loved her. Loved every single thing about her. Loved the way she made him feel.

"Are you bucking this event?" he asked. "I'll do your flank rope."

She shook her head. "Not this one. This one is all about you. And I'll be sitting out there when you're done to tell you *it's okay*, no matter what happens. Always."

Dead let off a shuddering breath. It released a hundred pounds of tension he hadn't even realized had settled over him in the past few weeks.

It's okay. Everything was okay.

"Are you ready?" she asked, gripping his shirt.

"To buck?"

She shook her head, and she looked so damn pretty in the light of his changing room, looking up at him like he was important. Like he was everything. "Ready for a life with me?"

He grinned. That was the easiest question in the world, but he wasn't going to answer it with a simple "yes." He wasn't going to answer like she expected. He was going to answer like she deserved.

Dead grinned down at her, gripped her waist, and then inhaled a deep, steadying breath because he'd never done this before. "I sure love you, Raven."

He would never forget her answering smile as long as he lived. This moment settled something tight in his chest. It freed him. When she whispered it back, he swore to all the stars he would never get tired of those words falling from her lips. He kissed her just to taste them.

She'd come into that rodeo arena a month ago and shook up his whole life. Shook up the herd, carved out her place with his friends, and took ownership of his heart and soul. And now she was lighting a fire in him to go and be the best because he could get her that ranch she wanted. She'd just kickstarted his motivation. He could help her save and build them a life that was good and fulfilling.

"You're ready to give up your old life and trust me to build another one?"

"I adored my old life," she murmured, "but I feel whole with you."

"Aawwww!" Two Shots called from the other side of the door.

Dead frowned at it. When he yanked the handle inward, the dumbass fell right to the floor by his feet.

Appalled, Dead glared at Cheyenne and Quickdraw, who were standing right outside, looking around at anything but Dead. "Were you guys spying on us?"

"Not spying. Cheering you on," Two Shots said, pushing up from the floor.

"Aren't you supposed to be bucking soon?" he demanded to Quickdraw.

"Oh, shit." The giant ran off and then reappeared in the doorway, skidding in the hallway dirt. "I hate Dead less when you're around," he told Raven.

Raven beamed, but Dead was at least fourteen percent offended. But before he could tell that asshole the statistics, Quickdraw had disappeared again.

"You said the L-word," Cheyenne crooned.

"Yeah, for Raven's ears only, and you guys ruined my moment."

"Want me to take a picture? For the next photobook?" Cheyenne held out her camera.

"No," Dead said at the same time Raven and Two Shots said, "Yes!" in unison.

They crowded him on either side, and Cheyenne snapped a picture. Dead was pretty sure his smile looked more like a grimace.

Why was Two Shots even in this picture?

"That one's going on your social media!" Cheyenne sang as she walked away.

Dead looked down at his nethers. "I don't have any pants on."

"I'll put a smiley face over your dangly bits."

"Dude, you told her you loved her for the first time while you were butt-naked," Two Shots said, clapping him on the back. "That's some confidence."

Raven had the mushiest smile on her face. "I think it was perfect."

"I didn't know she was coming here," he called out the door to Cheyenne and Two Shots' receding backs. "I would've got her flowers or pastie thingies! You know, those nipple stickers, but sparkly because heifers love sparkles. Or maybe cereal or something. I can be romantic!"

"I like that better than flowers," Raven said, pointing to his dick.

With a growl, he picked her up and wrapped her legs back around him, walked her toward the bathroom sink.

"Two minutes, Dead!" the handler yelled in the doorway.

Which scared the crap out of him so that he

almost dropped Raven, who was cracking up.

Dead cleared his throat and set her gently down in front of him to hide his boner. "Be right there!"

When Raven scurried toward the doorway, he reached out to yank her back in front of him. "No, no, no, no!" But she was too fast so he had to whip his hands in front of his boner.

Raven turned at the doorway, all sex appeal with her wicked sideways glance at him. "Dead, Dead, you're good in bed."

He canted his head. "You're so beautiful, Raven."

The smile faded slightly from her lips, and that pretty blush took her cheeks. "I don't want my old life anymore. I want this one. With you."

"You're sure?" He had to know he could make her happy. Had to hear it again.

"Dead, Dead, I choose you instead."

More Books in the Battle of the Bulls Series

Two Shots Down (Book 1)

Quickdraw Slow Burn (Book 3)

About the Author

T.S. Joyce is devoted to bringing hot shifter romances to readers. Hungry alpha males are her calling card, and the wilder the men, the more she'll make them pour their hearts out. She werebear swears there'll be no swooning heroines in her books. It takes tough-as-nails women to handle her shifters.

She lives in a tiny town, outside of a tiny city, and devotes her life to writing big stories. Foodie, wolf whisperer, ninja, thief of tiny bottles of awesome smelling hotel shampoo, nap connoisseur, movie fanatic, and zombie slayer, and most of this bio is true.

Bear Shifters? Check

Smoldering Alpha Hotness? Double Check

Sexy Scenes? Fasten up your girdles, ladies and gents, it's gonna to be a wild ride.

For more information on T. S. Joyce's work,
visit her website at
www.tsjoyce.com

Printed in Great Britain
by Amazon